Best Friends

Best Friends

Kira Chase

To order additional copies of this book, contact:
Xlibris Corporation
1-888-795-4274
www.Xlibris.com
Orders@Xlibris.com

TO THERESA (T.C. KNIGHT),
YOU'VE FILLED MY HEART AND SOUL WITH A JOY IT
HAS NEVER KNOWN. THE BEST IS YET TO COME.

SPECIAL THANKS TO:

Jennifer Loring, my wonderful editor

John Koviak for permission
to use his beautiful lyrics
YOU LIVE IN MY DREAMS,
who was inadvertantly
left out of the credits in ZINNA.

Janis and Eleonora
of Mario's Super Cuts - The Bronx

Chapter 1

Looking around the room at her fans amazed, and at the same time thrilled, Callie. She was pleased with herself for accomplishing what she'd set out to do with her latest book. Her goal to journey back to a traumatic but beautiful period of her life had come true. At times, she'd wondered if she should write it at all, but in the end she had to or she'd never have any peace. She'd had a steady following for her previous books, but wasn't certain how this one would be accepted, or how her peers and fans would perceive this mostly autobiographical period of her life, but the book, and she, had been warmly received, choking her with gratitude and heartfelt emotion. Her fans seemed to embrace her life, with many telling her it brought back bittersweet memories from their own first loves.

Callie scanned the crowd, waiting, hoping, wondering if by some miracle Katie'd seen the book, read it and would appear. Callie had even dedicated it to her. She'd traveled through countless cities, and the book tour was coming to an end with this being the last stop and in each city she prayed that Katie'd appear, but if she did Callie mused what her own reaction would really be. What would she say to someone she hadn't seen or talked to in over thirty years? What would Katie look like now? Had the years been kind to her? Where had her life taken her? Had she kept memories of what they'd once shared as close to her heart as Callie had? She closed her eyes and conjured up a beautiful image of them reuniting and stepping back into the magical world they once shared. A smile crossed her lips.

Callie had dedicated the book to her because of all the happiness and joy she'd brought into her life. Katie'd seen Callie at her best and at her worst, accepting her unquestionably, and it was only because of her that Callie had survived at all.

She longed to go back to that wonderful yet turbulent time and hold on for dear life to what she and Katie had shared. If she were given a chance to choose a time in her life to relive, that would be it, but given a second chance she would change both of their destinies. No woman since Katie had ever made Callie taste life so vividly and feel so loved and cared about, or brought so much passion and compassion to her life. Katie would always remain her friend and soul mate, but now she could only go back in her memory to that precious sacred time, that time that still played vividly in her mind and tormented her aching heart.

1967

Callie rushed off the school bus, then hurried inside the building to her locker. She quickly glanced around herself to make certain that no one saw her as she grabbed a bottle from behind some books stacked on the top shelf of her locker. She held the bottle to her lips and took a large swallow. The whiskey burned her throat but soothed her tortured soul. She had no choice—she needed it. It was as simple as that. Alcohol was the only thing that would get her through the day. She was fourteen years old.

Two of her friends headed up the hall towards her. She sighed. It was the same routine they followed every day—everything was routine here. They were stuck in a little corner of rural New York State—small-town Littledale, USA. Her friends would reach her locker, and they would follow their same monotonous ritual of walking down the corridor to the girls' room for a smoke before their first class.

Everything and almost everyone in this town was boring to

Callie nowadays. The housewives got up at dawn every morning and dutifully prepared breakfast, then sent their husbands off to one of the many furniture factories or railroad jobs, and shooed their children off to school. After their domestic chores were completed, the women huddled together like a bunch of old hens, squawking over the latest gossip as they swapped recipes. Then they'd rush home to greet their children and later their husbands.

They repeated the same routine day in and day out, but to look at them one got the impression that the women were actually content with their dull uneventful lives. Maybe some of them were, but Callie believed they were only brainwashed into thinking security lay in the fact that they were Mrs. Housewife. They modeled themselves after June Cleaver and Harriet Nelson with whatever dreams they may have dreamed when they were younger traded for the coveted title of Mrs. Anybody believing that anything was better than remaining single in society's eyes. Callie sought so much more out of life—excitement and adventure—but she doubted she'd get either from Littledale, the city that thrived on sameness as far as she was concerned. Oh, there was plenty to do here, but after awhile the dull rut set in, and that was the one thing that stifled her. She hated schedules and planning her life hour by hour, with a nine-to-five routine, or staying at home cooking, cleaning and devoting her life entirely to suit the needs of another while her own ambitions and self worth as a human being were swept aside. That would never suit her. She was on edge more than usual today. The restlessness that had seeped into her soul two years earlier had grown steadily worse.

Twelve had been a strange year for her, a year full of surprises and new awakenings. She had smoked her first cigarette, had her first beer and received her first kiss...from a girl...a little redhead named Jill who filled her with desires Callie never knew she possessed. She quickly fell head over heels in love with Jill, but she also learned a hard lesson: Don't tell your mother you're in love, especially if it's with the same sex. Shortly after proclaiming her love, Jill disappeared forever from her life. Callie suspected her mother had something to do with Jill's sudden disappearance from her life, even though nothing was ever said, but the realization remained that Jill had brought out something in her that couldn't be denied, just ignored for the time being.

Callie was a good student, studied hard and wasn't a troublemaker in school but still she despised school and cut classes as many times as she could get away with. Her extracurricular activities usually included smoking pot, drinking and popping pills, but she refused to shoot up and had little tolerance for anyone who did. She set her own high goals for herself with her dream to become a writer some day spending much of her time alone up in her room writing and listening to music. The music made her come alive and she'd practice dancing in front of the floor length mirror every night, consequently becoming a good dancer in the process.

Her home life was unbearable at times, but she was fed and clothed very well, and had a nice comfortable roof over her head. The one thing lacking from her life was the thing she craved most—love. Her mother never bonded with her, causing Callie to grow up with the impression that she was unlovable. She never confided her deepest feelings to anyone, but instead poured all of her pain into her writing with her diary becoming her most trusted friend. Her most secret thoughts and uncertainties about herself and her feelings, even though she thought she'd all ready accepted her differences, went into her diary. She kept the key hidden where no one would find it, then slid the diary behind some boxes on her closet shelf.

Callie couldn't ignore the feelings Jill had aroused within her, even though they'd shared nothing more than long sensual kisses. Those needy and foreign sensations Jill had brought out in her couldn't be denied and only filled Callie's mind with more confusion causing her to desperately force herself to feel the same way about boys that her friends did, but it was no use; no matter how hard she tried, boys just didn't stimulate her the way

Jill had and only left her feeling jaded and more determined to live the sexual part of her life apart from the opposite sex. She would never allow any male to feel superior over her, even though her friends told her, and appeared to accept the fact, that it was the only way to hold on to a guy. Callie seethed inside when she witnessed her friends acting like complete idiots around boys, feigning ignorance while the boys puffed out their chests reveling in their unearned self-importance.

She had some close male friends, and they were okay as friends only if they accepted just that from her, with no expectations of anything more. She couldn't tell her female friends that a boy was the last thing she wanted to hold on to, so she played the game and pretended to be like all the other girls. If anyone were to find out the true nature of her desires she'd be ridiculed and shunned by everyone with her fate becoming worse than death, but still, as hard as she tried, there was no changing that fact, so she locked her true feelings deep within her heart and even with her closest friends around her, she was lonely— terribly lonely—and that loneliness only added to her restlessness. She longed to unburden her heart to someone, but there was no one she trusted to understand so her secrets remained buried within her until hopefully the day would come when she'd find that special someone who possessed the same screwed-up feelings that she did. Only then would Callie begin to understand herself and find the joy she was sure waited for her somewhere in this big lonely world, but she doubted that special someone existed in Littledale.

Debbie Alison and Michelle Sturgis now stood in front of her. Callie slammed her locker shut then turned to them.

"Come on let's go," Michelle insisted. "If we don't go now we'll be late for class."

Callie took her usual place with Michelle in the middle and Debbie on Michelle's other side, and they headed down the long corridor to the girls' room. Michelle and Debbie chattered amongst themselves. It was the same thing they did every morning so

Callie tuned out the babbling and gazed at the familiar bodies milling up and down the hallway, or leaning up against lockers. Nothing changed, and nothing would ever change in Littledale and she was stuck in this time warp with people who either didn't like change or were afraid of it. Eighteen seemed like a lifetime away, but the minute she graduated from high school she was out of here one way or the other. This place suffocated her, and her only hope was to survive for the next four years.

Callie glanced at Michelle, who was intently listening to Debbie's ramblings. She'd met Michelle last year in the seventh grade. She sat behind Callie in homeroom, and they happily discovered they had a lot of the same classes together, not realizing at the time they shared the same classes only because their last name initials were the same. In high school they'd be separated into classes according to their abilities. Michelle was bright enough but didn't care about setting any goals for her life, which irritated Callie to no end. She was content to focus her energies on meeting the right boy and settling down after high school to a non-existent life as somebody's wife and raising a slew of rug rats. Michelle would carry on the legacy as the women of Littledale had for generations. That's all that was expected out of any girl in this town, but it wasn't for Callie, and she'd rather be dead right now than to believe that this was all destiny had in store for her. She was capable of taking care of herself, straight or gay, and would never depend on anyone for what she wanted or needed for her own life.

Callie already knew that when she reached the ninth grade she would be put in mostly advanced classes because she was intelligent, according to the tests she'd been given and her performance in junior high. She laughed, wondering why the administration even bothered putting girls in advanced classes when the only jobs the counselors geared them for, if the females insisted on a career, were as secretaries, nurses or schoolteachers, none of which appealed to her. Callie wanted to be a journalist, which she knew would aid her with her future writing career, but her guidance counselors, let alone her family, would never support her decision. Her family already ridiculed her dream to be a writer and it hurt deeply, but she'd be damned if she'd let them know. It was one more thing that separated her from her family.

Being in advanced classes had a stigma attached to it, and she didn't want to be labeled a freak just because she was smart. That label would hold her up to mockery, so she set out to show everyone that she could be smart and cool at the same time, and worked her ass off to project that image to the world—the world of Littledale anyway. Michelle and she became fast friends, and soon found themselves spending almost every weekend together going to movies, listening to records, partying on the riverbank with the older crowd, or hanging out at the local diner. Michelle shared Callie's passion for cigarettes, pot, and alcohol, but Callie didn't share Michelle's passion for chasing boys; she only pretended to, and hid her boredom enduring the long lazy weekend afternoons and early evenings cruising the streets in pursuit of these obnoxious specimens.

Michelle was plain with long blonde hair and a noticeable acne problem. Her two older brothers and sister made her family seem small in comparison to Callie's family and most of Callie's other friends' families. Michelle's family owned more cats than Callie had ever known anyone to own and was surprised that the cats all lived in the house with them. Callie's mother would have never allowed a pet to inhabit her home. The first time Callie'd been invited over she almost vomited from the stench inside the small cramped house, her nostrils burning from the foul odor. Michelle and her family seemed oblivious to the smell, but Callie surmised they'd probably grown accustomed to it and didn't even notice how offensive it was to their guests. She often thought about mentioning it to Michelle, but dismissed the idea when she couldn't come up with a tactful way to tell her. She'd gone to Michelle's house only a few times after that, but only out of politeness, feigning an excuse to leave after a few minutes.

One day when she witnessed the cats crawling on the kitchen

table and licking the butter in the butter dish, then afterward one of Michelle's brothers spreading some butter on a slice of bread, her stomach lurched; for weeks she was consumed with dry heaves whenever she even looked at a butter dish. When Michelle asked her why she never wanted to spend the night anymore, Callie's ready excuse was that she had her own bedroom and Michelle shared one with her older sister Carla and it just made more sense for Michelle to spend the night at her house so her sister didn't butt into their personal business, Michelle always agreed with her reasoning. Michelle reeked of the cats, though, and telltale hairs littered her clothing, but she had a nice personality and was genuinely fun to be with when Debbie wasn't around, but when Debbie was near, Michelle's personality took on a biting edge. Callie didn't totally dislike Debbie; there were times she was okay, but other times her tongue would cut like a razor. Callie couldn't understand why Michelle felt the need to impress Debbie, but for some odd reason she did, and would imitate Debbie's harsh tongue-lashings at innocent victims. Callie surmised that Michelle was a follower only to boost her own low self-esteem.

"What's up this weekend?" Michelle asked. "Going out with Jack again?"

Jack was Callie's boyfriend. She didn't have a chance to answer her before Michelle continued, "Or you hanging out with Dana?"

Callie shrugged as she nodded to some friends who passed them in the hall.

Debbie rambled on and on about some guy named Joey who had the hots for her. It was the same ritual. Callie seriously doubted any boy gave Debbie the time of day let alone had the hots for her, but to hear Debbie tell it she had more boyfriends than any girl in the school. Whenever she and Michelle or the rest of the crowd they hung with were supposed to meet one of her mystery men, Debbie instantly offered an apologetic excuse as to why the meeting couldn't take place. Callie would never tell her to her face that she thought she was a liar, but she knew deep in her heart that Debbie was, and she pitied her instead of becoming angry with her. Debbie Alison was a homely girl, not just plain but what Callie and her friends referred to as butt-ugly, with a wide mouth, big lips, buckteeth, mousy brown colored hair and a sallow complexion. Her boyfriends existed only in her imagination; Callie was certain of that fact, and she felt sorry for Debbie mostly because she heard the snickers and cruel whispers behind Debbie's back. Debbie's way to build her own self esteem was to run down almost every girl in the school whether she knew anything about them or not. As nasty as she could be, though, her loyalty knew no bounds if one of her friends were in dire need of something. She was as nasty as she was good.

"We're going out of town this weekend," Debbie beamed, looking at her.

Callie looked into her dull eyes. "Well, maybe we can meet him next time, Debbie," she answered with a weak smile.

Debbie nodded, then turned her attention and rambling mouth back to Michelle who, Callie observed, nodded every now and then since she couldn't get a word in edgewise.

They were almost to the end of the junior high hall, ready to turn the corner when Callie saw her. She was standing near the office with one shoulder leaning against the wall. Callie had never seen her around school before. Her heart lurched, surprising herself as she stared at the girl, barely realizing she was staring until the girl caught her eye and flashed her the most beautiful half-crooked smile Callie had ever seen and she self-consciously smiled back, her gaze quickly traveling over the stranger, taking in her lank but well-proportioned body.

She wore a plain jumper that went to the middle of her knees, with a classic white cotton blouse and navy blue knee socks that matched her jumper. Black flats adorned her feet. Callie's eyes met the girl's eyes again, and she felt an unexplainable quivering in her chest. Her smile was the warmest, friendliest smile Callie had ever seen, and she instinctively knew that it was sincere, making Callie's senses awaken as though she'd been in a deep slumber. She saw the girl's gaze sweep over her body, making Callie glad that she'd worn her favorite mini skirt showing much of her legs, which were long and curvy. The compliments Callie received on her legs made them one of her best assets.

"Come on, Cal, or we won't have time for a smoke, and Buckley will be pissed off if we're late again," Michelle whined.

Callie ignored her. "Who's that girl over there?"

Michelle and Debbie turned to where Callie was looking. "I don't know," Michelle shrugged. "Transfer, I guess."

"Looks like a hick to me," Debbie smirked.

Michelle chuckled. "Yeah, someone needs to show her how to dress."

Michelle's remark made Debbie laugh harder and louder. Callie noticed that the girl was watching them. Her gaze drifted from Callie to Michelle and Debbie, then back to Callie. Callie didn't join in Michelle and Debbie's laughter, and she hoped the girl saw that. She certainly didn't want her to think she was as rude and ignorant as her friends were. Callie remembered an old saying of her grandmother's about being careful with the company you keep because people judge you by the friends you associate with. She kept smiling at the girl but inside felt guilty for not admonishing Debbie and Michelle for their blatant ridicule of her. They knew nothing about her, and Callie felt like she was betraying this girl by keeping silent. *What an ass I'm being*, she thought, I *don't even know her either. I'll probably never see her again.* Callie nodded to the stranger, then followed Michelle and Debbie into the girls' room, but the girl's image stayed in her mind confusing Callie.

They passed a cigarette among themselves while Debbie babbled on about Joey and all the escapades they had been involved in. Callie had heard the same stories over and over so many times that she felt like pulling her hair out—or Debbie's. With each telling, though, Debbie inserted a different boy's name. Callie nodded politely, praying for the bell to ring—something she rarely did—and seconds later the shrill bell did sound, releasing her from Debbie's tedious monologue. "Well, I'm outta here," she said, and headed for the door.

"Yeah, I gotta get down to phys ed." Debbie tossed the cigarette butt into the toilet, then put her foot up on the handle and flushed, watching the butt swirl out of sight. "Catch you guys later."

"Wait up," Michelle yelled as Callie headed out the door. "So you don't wanna hang out this weekend?"

"I promised Dana I'd see a movie or something. I haven't hung out with her in a while." Dana had been Callie's closest friend for several years. She was a year older than Callie, but ever since Dana had entered high school, Callie didn't see much of her. A year apart, but it seemed like a world apart. It didn't matter that only a hallway separated them and they still rode the bus together, it was just that Dana was making new friends and joining activities that excluded junior high schoolers. They still liked to hang out when they could, though, and Callie was certain that once she herself entered high school they'd hang out more often, just like they used to.

"Okay, I'll call...maybe we can do something Sunday."

"Sure, whatever." She knew that Michelle would badger her off and on for the rest of the day about her weekend plans.

Chapter 2

All morning Katie Johnson wandered through the halls of her new school looking at the numbers on the classroom doors and finding herself late for almost every class. She wished she'd see the girl she'd seen this morning in one of her classes, but so far she hadn't. That girl had been the only one to even acknowledge her existence. She was finding her new classmates to be cold and unwelcoming. She hated Littledale.

She looked down at her clothes, wishing she would have worn something else today, but it had been so cool this morning that she'd assumed it'd be chilly all day. She'd never get used to the weather here. It was one more reason to loathe this place and yearn for the southern warmth and hospitality she loved and missed.

***

Callie sat through Buckley's class, barely paying attention to what he was muttering about. She stifled a yawn. She hated history class as much as she hated math class, and it wasn't long before her mind traveled elsewhere, which was nothing new for her as most of her waking hours seemed to be immersed in daydreaming. She couldn't focus, but she'd catch up later. When she was alone she'd study and get through; she always did.

The rest of the morning passed uneventfully and later in the cafeteria, during lunch, she joined the rest of her friends, sitting at the same table in the same places and having basically the same conversation day after day. She couldn't concentrate on anything anyone was saying. She couldn't get the girl with the crooked smile off of her mind. There was something about her that drew Callie to her and she couldn't explain what it was. She felt some invisible connection to her almost like an enormous surge of energy from an electrical current had seemed to pass between them when she first laid eyes on the stranger. No one had ever had such a powerful impact on her, and it frightened and confused her at the same time.

"What the hell's the matter with you?" Michelle inquired annoyed. "I've asked you the same thing three times!"

She turned to her friend. "Huh? I'm sorry. I'm...I'm just not with it today."

"Problems?"

"No...no."

"Boy problems?" Debbie knowingly asked. "You and Jack have a fight?"

"No. Everything's cool. We're fine."

"You gonna see him this weekend?" Debbie asked.

"Uh-uh."

Her eyes grew wide. "Why? You're going steady."

"And I have a life," Callie said a little too sharply. "My whole world doesn't revolve around Jack Busman."

"God, what're you, on the rag today?" She angrily took a bite out of an apple.

Callie exhaled noisily as she looked at Debbie. "I'm sorry...I've just got a lot on my mind." She took a couple bites from her sandwich, then tossed it back in the bag. She looked around the cafeteria, listening to the music blaring from two large speakers attached to the back wall. That was the one good thing about lunchtime—the music. It was a miracle that the establishment allowed them to play music during their lunch break when they still separated the boys from the girls during lunch. She smiled to herself. The boys' cafeteria was on the other side of the hall and it was just as well with Callie, because adolescent boys were pigs as far as she was concerned. She had five brothers to confirm that fact and she often referred to them as her pig brothers.

Her eyes searched the room, hoping to see the girl she'd seen this morning. With three lunch periods, she might not even be scheduled for this one, she realized. She was bored with the mundane senseless babbling; her gaze continued roaming tables of girls until finally two tables over she caught sight of her. Her breath caught in her throat when she saw her, and it took her a few seconds to realize that the stranger was looking at her with a bemused expression on her face. She wondered how long the girl's eyes had been focused on her. Callie shot her a faint smile, her face flushing slightly.

Terry Brace nudged her. "Who the hell you smiling at? You've got a goofy grin on your face."

Callie's face flushed. "Huh? Oh nothing. I just saw that new girl again."

"Oh, the cool one," Debbie snickered, craning her neck to get a view.

"What new girl?" Terry asked.

Callie ignored Terry's question. "We don't even know her, Debbie. You shouldn't say that."

"Well look at her," Michelle laughed.

Terry glanced in the direction everyone was now looking. "Oh, her. Yeah, she's in one of my classes. Real quiet."

"What's her name?" Callie asked.

"I don't know. She talks so low I didn't catch it."

"She's making a fashion statement," Michelle giggled. "Check out the knee socks!" She got the others at the table laughing with her. "Oh, she is so hot!"

Callie stood up.

"Where you going?" Michelle asked.

"You are so mean; she's sitting all alone. God, somebody should say something to her."

"Like what?" Michelle asked.

"Anything. At least make her feel like she's part of the school, welcome her or something. I mean, how would you feel if you were at a new school and were just totally ignored?"

Debbie and Michelle nudged each other. "Hopefully we'd be dressed a little better. We wouldn't look like Miss Hillbilly here. If we did, then we wouldn't expect anyone to talk to us either," Debbie giggled.

"Oh, like you two know so much about fashion?" She looked at Michelle's skirt, knowing that last year it belonged to her sister Carla, and Debbie's mini skirt emphasized the thickness of her thighs. "Coming?" she asked no one in particular.

"No," they answered in unison.

"Fine." She angrily squared her shoulders.

"Well, there goes Cal, always helping the underdog, taking another one under her wing." Debbie plopped her face in her hands.

Callie whirled around. "Look, I'm just trying to be friendly; nothing wrong with being nice to people." She would have said more, but she'd be wasting her breath on the likes of Debbie. She'd gone into her cruel mode and unfortunately, the new girl was her target.

***

Katie watched the girl who'd given her such a warm friendly smile this morning. She was the only one who'd offered her any kindness at all the entire morning. She couldn't understand how people could be so cold and uncaring. At her old school if there was a new student they were greeted with the friendly hospitality she missed so much now. She longed for the security of her friends and home back in Virginia, but circumstances beyond her mother's control brought them here to this bitter, unfriendly area of the universe. She pleaded with her mother to stay in the south, but her mother believed that more opportunities awaited them in the north. She'd never fit in here and would never get used to the cold shoulder she was getting and knew she'd never learn to like it here no matter how hard she tried. The only decent thing in Littledale was the mountains that surrounded the valley, reminding her of the mountains of Virginia. She had a beautiful view of them from her bedroom window, where she would stand and, closing her eyes, imagine she was back home. She swallowed the lump in her throat.

Katie watched as the girl talked with her friends noting how pretty she was, with long reddish brown hair. Her stylish short skirt showed off her long curvy legs, and Katie had been taken aback when she saw those legs this morning as she watched the girl and her friends walking down the hallway. Her own outfit was mismatched and definitely not in style, but style was something she didn't spend much time thinking about. A pair of jeans or cutoffs and a tee shirt or flannel shirt was her preferred mode of dress.

The girl looked at her and smiled. Katie smiled back watching the girl suddenly rise from the table, looking upset. Katie wished she could hear what the girl was saying to her friends. The girl looked back at her and flashed her another smile.

***

Callie walked over to the girl's table and sat down across from her. "Hi, I saw you this morning. I'm Cal. Is it okay if I sit here?" She flashed her a brilliant smile. "Welcome to our school."

She nodded. "Hi, I'm Katie."

Her voice was soft and low, but it was her smile that tugged at Callie's heartstrings as she witnessed the relief that washed over the girl's face. Callie assumed that she was relieved that someone was finally befriending her. She herself had never had to sit alone during lunch and imagined how lonely it must be, but then, everything about school must be lonely for this girl since everyone was a stranger to her. Callie knew it would be hard for her if she had to go to a strange school where no face was familiar. "So, what do you think of this wonderful institution of ours?" she laughed, keeping her eyes focused on the girl's beautiful face.

She shrugged. "I don't know...I guess...uh...people aren't very friendly around here. Maybe things will get better."

Callie noticed the southern twang and smiled. It wasn't real thick, but still very noticeable. She liked it. "Yeah, don't mind them." She waited for Katie to respond, but she remained silent, making Callie assume she was just shy. "So, do you have any trouble with your schedule? I'd be glad to help you out."

Katie smiled gratefully as she thrust the list of classes she'd been assigned to towards Callie. "Oh cool. Your next class is the same as mine. You can go with me if you want to." She looked into Katie's big green eyes, hoping she'd say yes, as a tremor went through her body.

"Thank you. I've been late for every class so far trying to figure this thing out." She frowned.

Callie liked the faint sprinkling of freckles across Katie's nose and her shoulder-length blondish hair with flecks of red. It was parted on the side with her bangs grown out to the length of her hair, which enabled her to sweep them to one side. She was void of any makeup, but had the type of skin that didn't really need any, but just the same, Callie wondered what she'd look like with some. Her cheekbones were high and she had perfectly spaced big green eyes and full lips, but it was her smile that commanded Callie's attention.

"So, you just move in or something?" She leaned her elbows on the table.

She nodded. "Yeah. My Mom lost her job so we moved here."

"What about your Dad?"

Her eyes drifted from Callie's. "I...My Dad doesn't live with us. My Mom and him are divorced."

Callie was surprised Katie'd shared that personal tidbit with her a virtual stranger. The town gossips would have a field day with her mother. The women of Littledale wouldn't socialize with any woman who was divorced. A widow was bad enough, forcing the married women to keep tighter reigns on their husbands, but trusting a divorced woman around their men was strictly out of the question. It was 1967, but it might as well have been 1867. Her marital status would exclude Katie's mother from most social activities, and Katie most likely would be taboo, too. Divorce just wasn't accepted in a backward society like this and Callie surmised that it probably was due to the women of Littledale being insecure and afraid how they would stand up next to someone from the outside, especially if the outsider was cultured or young and good-looking. "So, Katie, uh…what kinds of things do you like to do?"

"I like to fish," she quickly answered, eyes brightening.

Callie smiled at the way she pronounced fish. It sounded like "feesh." "Okay."

"You don't fish?"

"Not really. I tried it once a couple of years ago, but it didn't turn out to be a very pleasant experience." She raised her eyebrows. "To make a long story short, when I saw the fish wiggling on the end of my line, I ended up falling off the dock. That was enough for me."

Katie laughed.

"My brothers fish, though. Do you have any brothers or sisters?"

"No, just me and my Mom."

"I have five brothers and four sisters. Feel free to take any of them at any time."

She laughed again.

"My Dad died when I was a little kid so I don't have a father around either. Um, so what else do you like to do besides fish?"

She propped an elbow on the table. "Well, I like riding my bike, walking and hiking. I love the outdoors," she answered enthusiastically, "especially the mountains."

"So do I. What kind of music do you like?"

"Oh, just about everything."

"Same here, but not too much country…bluegrass is okay."
The warning bell sounded. Callie stood up. "Let me go throw my
garbage away and I'll be right back."

"Okay."

She walked back to her usual table. Her friends were on
their feet gathering the remnants of their lunches.

"Come on, let's go or we're gonna be late," Michelle said.

"I'll catch up. I promised the new girl, her name's Katie by
the way, that I'd walk with her to show her where the class is.
She's in our class, Michelle. She seems nice. Do you want to
walk with us?"

"Don't you mean that the other way around?" she snapped.

Callie shrugged. "You know what I meant." She saw the look
that passed between Debbie and Michelle. "Fine, forget it," she
said, giving them her most disgusted look. "You know, you two
really make me sick sometimes." She picked up her books and
walked back over to Katie, who stood waiting for her. "Are you
ready?"

Katie glanced over at Michelle and Debbie. "Are your friends
upset or something?" She hesitated.

"When aren't they? It has nothing to do with you," she
promptly assured her, even though their rudeness had everything
to do with Katie.

Callie kept her eyes focused on Katie during class. She sat
at the front of the room, and Callie sat in her customary location
in the back of the room with Michelle ever glued to her side.

"So what'd you find out about Katie?" Michelle whispered.

"She's cool," Callie whispered back.

"Give me a break…she's not hanging out with us," she said
disgustedly. "She doesn't fit in."

"She didn't ask to hang out with us," Callie stiffly replied.
"Besides, what makes you think she'd want to hang out with
you?" Michelle was jealous that she'd found a new friend and
felt threatened by it. "But you could give her a chance. You
might even see what a nice person she really is."

"Well, she's not going to get the chance. That's all I'm gonna say."

Katie was called on and stuttered, "I ain't got the answer to that, Ma'am."

Callie's heart went out to her as she watched Katie's bent head looking down at the book on her desk.

Michelle joined her fellow classmates in laughter at Katie's lack of command of proper English. "God, Debbie's right about her...she's so backwards, it's a wonder she can find her way anywhere."

Callie longed to run up to Katie and drag her out of the classroom, away from the taunting, but she could only sit at her desk, gaze riveted on the back of Katie's head. The knot in her stomach tightened as her anger mounted.

She ignored Michelle during the rest of the class, and when the bell rang, she watched as Katie grabbed her books and quickly headed out the door. She wanted to tell her that everything would be all right, but she wouldn't see Katie again until the last class of the day, which was English. Unfortunately, Michelle was in the remainder of her classes. Callie was hurt and ashamed by the way Michelle was acting. Michelle must have picked up on her feelings; she didn't try to engage her in conversation as they left the class, but walked in silence next to her to the girls' room. Once inside Callie took out her small gold lighter and lit a cigarette.

"Gimme a drag." Michelle said, breaking her silence as she pulled the cigarette from Callie's lips.

"Wait a damn minute," Callie snapped.

"Excuse me." Michelle angrily puffed away. "What the hell's the matter with you today?"

She eyed her sharply. Michelle knew what was wrong, but if she sincerely didn't then she was stupider than Callie thought. "I just think it's rotten to pick on someone you don't even know. You're not even giving her a chance."

"Well, if you think she's so wonderful, why don't you hang

out with her? I told you she doesn't fit in with us. No one wants her around…she's weird."

"Who the fuck do you think you are to dictate who can hang out with anyone? I don't see you winning any popularity contests. You can go to hell." Callie grabbed the cigarette back from her, took a few quick drags, then tossed it in the toilet. "It'd be different if you knew her. You never even talked to her, so what the fuck are you judging her for? This is her first day here and you're not even giving her a break."

"She's a hick."

Callie laughed sarcastically. "We're considered hicks, too, because we live in Littledale. Or have you forgotten?"

"It's not the same," Michelle indignantly shot back. "I don't know why you're defending her so much."

Callie threw her hands up. "I feel sorry for you." She stomped out of the girls' room.

***

Callie remained indifferent toward Michelle for the remainder of the day impatiently waiting for English class. Before class she didn't bother going to the girls' room for a smoke, but instead went straight to the classroom arriving early—something unusual for her—hoping to spot Katie the minute she walked in. She watched her classmates filing in, but didn't see Katie.

Michelle entered the room stomping over to her desk. "Where were you?" she snapped. "I turned around and you were gone."

Callie shrugged arching an eyebrow. "I wanted to get here early. I had to check my homework."

"Right," she said acerbically, plopping into the seat next to Callie's. "So where's your new friend? Maybe she ran home to her mommy or back to whatever hick place she came from," she smirked.

Callie disregarded her comments as she kept her eyes focused on the door. Mr. Pryor walked in and closed the door. She frowned.

Where was she? Maybe she should have waited in the hall for her and shown her the way to class. Minutes later the door opened and Katie timidly entered the room, looking embarrassed as all eyes riveted on her.

"Sit anywhere you'd like," Mr. Pryor motioned with an outstretched hand. "What's your name?"

"Katie Johnson," she answered in a barely audible voice.

But it was loud enough for Callie to hear. Now she knew her last name. She watched Katie's eyes scan the room for an empty seat and quickly raised her hand, trying to get Katie's attention, and when Katie finally looked her way Callie motioned to her. She smiled, then hurried to the empty seat on Callie's left side.

"Give me a break," Michelle muttered, slumping down in her seat.

Callie shot her a warning look, then turned her attention back to Katie. She looked pained and Callie felt sorry for her, but it wasn't in a pitying sort of way; she was sorry that her friends were so vindictive toward someone they didn't even know. They were acting like assholes, and Callie definitely didn't want Katie to think that everyone here acted that way—especially her.

She scribbled her phone number on a piece of paper, then quickly passed it to Katie, keeping her gaze glued on her, as Katie unfolded the slip of paper and read the message. A broad grin broke over Katie's face as she took a piece of paper from her notebook and scribbled a reply, then passed the note to her. Callie smiled as she read Katie's phone number then slipped the paper into her purse.

Michelle whispered, "What's going on? What are you two passing notes about?"

Callie didn't answer her, but glanced up at Mr. Pryor, who gave her a stern look. Self-consciously she looked down at her book. A few minutes later a note landed with a loud thud on her desk. She looked up to see Mr. Pryor with the same disapproving look, his eyes focused sharply on her. *It isn't fair*, she thought. He hadn't even look at Michelle, and she was the one who threw the note on her desk. "Knock it off, Michelle," Callie hissed, ignoring the crumpled note. "I'll talk to you after class." Mr. Pryor stared at her for a few more seconds, then turned his attention back to the blackboard. Callie hurriedly scribbled another note to Katie. *We can talk a little while after school if you want to.* She slipped it to her. Moments later another one came back to her. *I'd like that*, Katie had written. *I'm sorry that you almost got in trouble.*

Callie felt Michelle's eyes burning through her, knowing that Michelle was dying to know what Katie had written to her, and obviously wondering why Callie was acting so strangely. Ironically, Callie was wondering the same thing about herself, but she couldn't explain it to anybody; she was confused. Something unique connected her to Katie the instant their eyes first met, but she didn't know what it was. Katie Johnson was worth standing up for and fighting for—that was all she knew. She was risking a lot for Katie, but it was a risk worth taking. She'd always taken people under her wing and befriended those who appeared friendless until they began to make friends on their own, but it was different with Katie. Callie was wearing her heart on her sleeve, and she had to be careful lest anyone noticed, especially Katie. She'd fallen fast and hard for her and she didn't know what to do about it. This was the first time she'd ever felt an attraction towards a classmate and it made her feel sick and happy at the same time.

When the bell rang, Katie stayed in her seat and waited until Callie stood up before standing herself. "Where's your locker?" Callie asked.

Katie smiled. "It's…"

"Hey, wanna have a smoke before your bus comes? That is, if you have the time." Michelle asked sarcastically, cutting Katie off as though she weren't even there.

"No, I'm going to talk to Katie for a bit to make sure that she finds everything on Monday."

"Suit yourself." Michelle's eyes smoldered as she flashed a

dirty look at Katie. Katie's eyes drooped, but before Callie could say anything Michelle was rushing down the hall, the slant of her shoulders giving testimony to her anger. Callie knew Michelle couldn't wait to get home to call everybody and tell them how she had shoved her off for Katie, but Michelle would be over her ugly mood before the weekend was over. One thing about Michelle was that her anger never lasted long.

"Why doesn't she like me?"

"She's being a bitch. By picking on you, she thinks it makes her look cool. That's why she does it. Believe me she never used to be this way, and it just shows you how immature some people can be."

Her eyebrows furrowed. "So why do you hang with her?"

Callie sighed. "Lately I've been asking myself that same question." She had no truthful answer to give her. "Don't let her get to you. She's only hurting herself by losing out on the chance to make new friends."

"I don't want to cause any problems between you and your friends."

"Nobody chooses my friends for me. Besides, I like talking to you. You're a nice change of pace." She was pensive for a moment as she looked into Katie's bright eyes. "I'm a writer, you know, and I like to study people and try to figure out what makes them tick. If it's somebody I already know and they have this boring life, then I invent an exciting new life for them." She laughed awkwardly.

"You're a writer?" Katie's eyes grew wide. "That's cool. I never knew a writer before. Do you have stuff in magazines or books out?"

Callie frowned sheepishly. "Well, not yet, but someday I will. That's why I'm so curious about people. I thought about writing a book about the people in this town. Kinda like a *Peyton Place*." She rolled her eyes. "Uncover all those deep dark secrets. Just wait till you meet some of Littledale's finest."

Katie laughed. "You're so funny."

"That's me," she grinned. "So where's your locker?"

"Down the hall."

"You don't talk much do you?"

She shrugged. "I suppose not. Only when I got something to say."

Callie beamed as they walked in silence down the corridor. Getting Katie involved in a conversation consisting of more than a few short replies was going to be like pulling teeth. She herself was a talker and usually was accused, by those who knew her well, of dominating every conversation. She yearned to learn about the life Katie had before she came to Littledale, and especially why she'd ended up in this hellhole of all places on earth, but Callie didn't want to appear to be nosy, so she kept her questions to herself for now. If she and Katie became friends, she was certain that in time Katie would answer all of those questions.

Katie's locker was situated at the opposite end of the hall from Callie's. Katie opened it, placed her books inside, grabbed some others, and her homework assignments, then closed the door.

Callie wondered if the reason Katie wasn't talking much was because of the way she'd been snubbed all day, or maybe if she was just shy. She hoped Katie didn't think she'd turn out to be like the others. She desperately needed Katie to know that she wasn't like everyone else. "So, what're you gonna do this weekend? It's supposed to be nice out."

She bit her bottom lip. "I dunno. Probably help my Mom settle the apartment. It's been hard on her this week."

"When did you move in?"

"Last weekend."

Callie's eyebrows shot up as she leaned against the locker. "So if you moved in last weekend, how come you didn't come to school till today?"

Her eyes narrowed. "We had to wait for my records to get transferred from my other school."

"Oh." Callie wished Katie would ask her some questions, but she didn't. "Well, wanna go to my locker with me if you have the time? I don't want your Mom to be worried or upset if you're late getting home."

A faint smile crossed her lips. "She won't. She works crazy hours, and every day is a different schedule. I spend a lot of time by myself." Her eyes drifted from Callie's, but not before Callie saw the loneliness and sadness in them.

"You mean nobody's there when you come home from school?" she asked, leading the way to her locker.

"Sometimes she's there, but it depends on her shift since she's a waitress."

"Where does she work?"

She laughed. "I don't remember the name of the town. I have the phone number written down in case of an emergency, though." She cocked her head. "I'll never remember the names of these towns," she added almost apologetically.

"Sure you will, but until you do if you ever need anything give me a call. Okay? I take it you live close to school? If not, I hope I didn't make you miss your bus. But don't worry, if you did, I'll make sure you get home all right."

"I walk."

"Where do you live?"

"Not far…near the river."

"That'll be good for you since you love to fish. My brothers fish this end of town a lot."

She nodded.

"It's too bad you and Michelle don't get to know each other. She lives in that area. You could walk to school together. Do you know where The Projects are? She lives near them." She watched Katie's face suddenly fall. "Do you live near there?" They reached Callie's locker and Callie opened the door, dumping her books inside.

"Not too far from here," she quickly answered as she fidgeted with a book cover.

"Well, if you want, give me a call and we can do something this weekend. I can show you around."

"Where do you live?" she abruptly asked.

"Let's see. I don't know how much you've seen of the town. You know where downtown is?" she asked, grateful that Katie had finally asked her a question about herself.

"Uh-uh."

"Okay, you know right at the end of Main Street before the underpass there's a street right next to the Hyland Hotel. I live on that street there—Crescent Street—in the first house on the right next to the big parking lot. The A&P is the first building on the left. In fact, I can look out my bedroom window and see everyone coming down the street or into the parking lot."

Her eyes widened. "So you really are downtown."

"Yeah," she grinned. "Sometimes I walk home from school when it's nice out. I would've today, but I didn't feel like it." She wasn't being totally honest, but she couldn't tell Katie that she'd practically sell her soul just to have a few minutes alone with her. She was categorically infatuated and needed to keep a level head on her shoulders. She couldn't let Katie see the effect she had on her; it was much too dangerous.

"Big weekend plans?"

"No, just the usual. I'm going to see a James Bond movie with one of my friends tonight. I don't know what I'll do the rest of the weekend," she replied, hoping that Katie might suggest getting together.

"I hope she doesn't give you a hard time for helping me out today. She's pretty mad at you."

"No, I'm not going to the movie with Michelle, I'm hanging out with a friend named Dana. She's a year ahead of us. If you want, sometime I'll introduce you around to everybody. You'll feel better once you make some friends." She smiled warmly at her. "I'm sorry that your first day was so rotten, but I'm glad I got to meet you, Katie."

"Even though I made a fool out of myself in class?" she asked in a low voice.

She shrugged. "Don't worry about it. They're just being as

swipes…you didn't do anything wrong. And I really am glad I got to meet you," she said again.

Katie grinned. "Thanks. You've made this day not so bad."

Callie wished she could think of something witty to say, but words escaped her. "Now I guess I'll go out back and have a smoke before the bus comes. Do you smoke?"

She nodded.

"Cool. Do you want to have one now?"

"I'd better get home."

"Okay. I'll see you Monday then, unless you wanna do something together this weekend. Just give me a call."

"Okay." She smiled again. "Bye."

"Bye, Katie." Callie slammed her locker shut then watched Katie make her way down the hall and open the door and slip outside into the bright sunlight. She fought the urge to run after her and ask her what invisible hold she had over her. She was in agony and she didn't know what to do about it. She hated being different from other girls, and she hated herself for the thoughts that were going through her mind right now about Katie. She had to maintain her cool and be on guard around Katie, struggling against the desire to touch her and feel the comfort of her warm flesh next to her own. Katie's dizzying effect on her made her pulse quicken and her breath shorten. These emotions scared her into an almost paranoid state. She stood for a few minutes, taking several deep breaths, then slowly let them out as she walked down the hall.

Chapter 3

Callie's mother confronted her the minute she walked in the door, standing in her usual 'you're in trouble' stance with arms crossed over her chest. "What?" Callie asked. She knew a lecture was coming but didn't know which one it would be this time. She racked her brain, but didn't recall any incidents lately that would invoke her mother's wrath, but most times her mother didn't offer an explanation and Callie stood confused and angry as she became the unwitting victim to her mother's rage. Her mother's values weren't always the opposite of her own, even though that's what Mrs. Stone appeared to believe most of the time. Or Callie wondered if maybe it made her mother feel better to label her a radical even though she certainly didn't feel like one. She believed in honesty, sincerity, and helping those less fortunate, but her mother never seemed to focus on her good qualities, only her mistakes. Callie's failures and disappointments seemed to please her, and she appeared to derive pleasure in making Callie's life miserable, so Callie unquestionably accepted the communication gap between she and her mother doubting things would ever get better between them. Her mother's anger and coldness toward her was never made clear to Callie. All Callie knew for certain was that her mother harbored a bitterness against her without reason, so Callie wondered how she could be expected to change a character flaw in herself if she had no clue as to what the supposed flaw was. Their mother-daughter rift widened with each passing day.

Ever since she could remember Callie had felt like an outsider in her own home finding it strange to live in a house with so many siblings but having absolutely nothing in common with them. She felt ganged up on, like the runt being unmercifully tormented and taunted most of the time, so she threw herself into her solitary endeavors. When she looked to her mother for support she received none and realized that her mother believed anything her brothers and sisters told her. Consequently, Callie often found herself unjustly punished for things she'd never even thought of doing. No one knew, or even if they did, cared about the pain she carried inside. Being innocent until proven guilty didn't exist in her home, at least not where she was concerned anyway. Her older brothers were okay—the ones in Viet Nam—but her older sister was her biggest problem. She'd dropped out of high school and sat around the house, friendless by both sexes until a chance meeting with the friend of one of her brothers. He was the first guy who'd given her any attention—and his dick. It was only a matter of time before she came to their mother in tears announcing her pregnancy. But that was all right in Mrs. Stone's eyes, and Lorraine's mistake would be rectified. She would be married off before the baby came, and no one would be the wiser.

"Heard they checked lockers for drugs," Lorraine said mockingly.

Callie rolled her eyes. "So. It has nothing to do with me." She wasn't in the mood for a fight. She was happy, and that was a feeling she rarely experienced. For once there was a light in her life, and she'd be damned if her sister was going to dim it. "Besides, it was only one pothead's locker. They only busted him because he was selling grass on school grounds. He's an idiot."

Lorraine eyed her warily. "You're probably taking drugs," she smugly accused. "You run around every weekend, and no one knows where you go or who you're with. You're getting a reputation."

Callie smirked. "Yeah, right. My friends are all druggies. I shoot up a hundred times a day with them." She held her bare arms straight out. "Just look at all my needle tracks. Oh, don't mind my collapsed veins."

Mrs. Stone eyed her antics with disgust. "You'd better watch that mouth of yours," she warned.

"Too bad you didn't tell her what to watch," Callie flippantly replied.

A sharp crack across Callie's cheek ended any more comments she may have had. She looked evenly at her mother, her cold dark eyes boring into her own. Her mother wanted her to cry or yell out in pain, but she'd never give her the satisfaction. A self-righteous look was evident on her mother's face. Callie sniffed indignantly, knowing Lorraine and her mother would spend the next hour discussing the possibilities of whether Callie was or wasn't taking drugs and what should be done about it.

She shot them both a look of indifference, then walked upstairs where she would find peace in the quietness and sanctity of her bedroom. She tried to get close to her mother, but her efforts were futile, especially when Lorraine was around. Even though her mother was worried about her three brothers in the Marines, she wished she could see that she was worried, too, and a couple of times a month she sent letters and care packages to each of them at her own expense. Her mother never commented about her good deeds seeming never to see anything good in her, especially her sensitive side, or if she did see anything worthy, she pretended that she hadn't. Callie doubted her mother ever would see how much good there truly was inside of her, and she would never understand why she was the black sheep of the family, and would always wonder what it was about her that warranted such hostility.

She wanted just once in her life to hear her mother say 'I love you,' or to make her feel like she was truly wanted and belonged. But Mrs. Stone never did. Even as a young child Callie would lie in her bed, listening to her mother telling the others good night, then hear her gently kissing their cheeks. She never came near Callie's bed, and Callie believed that she must be the most horribly unlovable little girl in the world if her own mother couldn't even bear to kiss her goodnight. Night after night, the loneliness engulfed her as hot heavy tears flowed from her eyes. Callie didn't hate her mother, though; she just didn't know her and her mother made no attempt to want to get to know her.

Even though Callie was concerned about her brothers in the Viet Nam War, she still agonized about the usual things teenagers agonized about—except when it came to boys. She looked at her reflection in her bureau mirror. She'd gotten a very short haircut the previous winter and it was finally growing out, and she wanted it to grow as long as it could, hardly being able to wait to ditch the bangs and part her hair in the middle. She hoped by the end of summer her hair would be a length she could comfortably live with.

She prayed that her family would respect her differences and opinions instead of always encumbering her with theirs, expecting her to do and like the same things they did. Different was good, but they refused to see that, and tried to mold her into a clone of what they thought she should be, but she would never compromise her own beliefs.

She hated school dances and had only gone to one once in the seventh grade because of her mother's nagging. She found it dull and unexciting and never went to another. She shied away from extracurricular school activities; she had nothing in common with the kids who encompassed the various groups. Her social life revolved around drinking and partying with her friends. In her dark moods, which sometimes seemed to engulf her, she wrote hauntingly passionate poetry and prose about the unfairness and absurdity of life. She pored over books on astrology, the black arts, and religion, anything that would give her the answers she sought, trying in vain to figure out what her life was really all about and why she even existed, but finally came to the simple conclusion that one's life, no matter how desperate, simply had to be lived and gotten through. That was all there was to it. Maybe the meaning and reason for human existence would never be truly known in life, only when the life had drained from the body and the cold clamminess of death had crept in would the answers be revealed.

Her life had always been harsh, with things happening to her that she was certain weren't happening to her friends or her siblings, but Katie might now add a buffer to her adolescent angst. She wanted Katie in her life, but at the moment, she didn't know how much she needed her.

Callie grabbed her notebook and tried to write but found concentrating difficult, so she turned on her record player. She still couldn't get Katie off her mind. There was something about her that gripped her heart and haunted her soul, making her feel weak-kneed around her, but she could never let Katie see the effect she was having on her. She worried about making her emotional weakness too obvious to her friends, and especially to Katie, and it tortured her soul. She closed her eyes and Katie's vision swam before her. She wiped perspiration from her brow, feeling sick. It wasn't a sickness she was familiar with; she was lovesick. It'd come unexpectedly out of the blue and zapped her before she knew what was happening. Her feelings frightened her, making her feel out of control. She knew nothing about Katie Johnson, but still she felt pulled toward her.

Whenever she heard the telephone ring, she opened her bedroom door and listened, hoping to be summoned. The only times she was called was when Jack phoned to say he'd miss her over the weekend, and Dana called to say she was on her way over with Grace Reed. How Callie wished it had been Katie calling her. The sound of Katie's voice was like music to her ears, and she wanted to hear her voice again and again.

Dana and Grace arrived about seven. Callie didn't care much for Grace, finding her disposition one of assuming that the world owed her something. *She wasn't bad looking and she might even be attractive if she'd shed some weight—like fifty pounds*, Callie thought. Grace was too obnoxious for Callie's liking, and she only tolerated her for Dana's sake. She made amicable, polite conversation with her, sensing that she wasn't one of Grace's favorite companions either. Callie couldn't comprehend what Dana and Grace had in common, but she supposed that Dana felt that way about some of her friends, too, because she'd never been too enthusiastic about getting together with Michelle or Debbie. Dana was blonde, petite, and pretty with a sweet personality, making her popular with both boys and girls. Callie doubted that Dana had an unkind bone in her entire body.

In the darkened movie theater Callie tried to force her eyes and mind to stay focused on the movie, but finding it fruitless, finally closed her eyes and let her imagination take her on a passion filled fantasy shared with Katie. She smiled to herself in the shadowy theater, safe in the embrace of its protecting arms as her emotions consumed her soul. When the movie ended and the lights came up, she felt let down, knowing that she was once again thrust into the real world, away from the fantasies that had given her so much short-lived comfort. She hated those feelings of attraction towards Katie, knowing Katie would probably avoid her like the plague if she suspected, but she was powerless over the commotion inside of her and wished she had someone to share her confusion with and to help her make some sense of it.

She followed Dana and Grace outside, noting the night had taken on a chill, but her flesh still felt warm, the flush spreading throughout her body. She tried to beg off going to the diner for a Coke, but finally relented and spent the next hour listening to the boy talk she so much despised. She was relieved when the evening ended and she parted company with Dana and Grace.

Arriving home, she was disappointed to learn there were no messages waiting for her. She'd convinced herself all evening that Katie would call. She wondered what Katie was doing tonight. She should call her, but fear gripped her heart. She didn't want to appear pushy. She wished Katie would make the first move toward friendship, but what if she didn't? She tried to put her thoughts into the proper perspective and be rational, but Katie's magnetism overpowered her usual sensibilities. They'd only met today and maybe Katie didn't want her friendship and was only friendly to her in school because no one else offered her any help. After she made some friends, Callie was certain that Katie would most likely go her own way with a different crowd, and it would only be a matter of time with her looks before she found a boyfriend. That thought disturbed Callie, and she quickly banished it from her mind. She didn't know which way to turn or what to do. She wanted Katie to think she was cool, but if she called her, Katie might see how vulnerable she really was. All Callie knew was that she longed to be near her and kept reliving how she'd felt being next to her this afternoon. Those earlier stirrings she'd felt intensified and she couldn't stop them. She'd felt those same stirrings when she was twelve and Jill's lips had met hers for the first time.

She yearned to talk to someone about her strange desires, but there was no one she could trust. How could she possibly explain the chaos churning inside of her? Who would understand these unnatural feelings? Everyone would think she was a pervert, and she didn't want to be locked up with crazy people or sent to a convent; she just wanted to understand why she felt this way and needed to know if any other girls had these same odd feelings and desires, but most of all she needed to know why had she been chosen to be different. It was a living hell; she felt alone and numb, set apart from the rest of the world. She doubted her friends suspected her attraction to girls and she worked hard to keep their suspicions at bay.

She'd never been attracted to a classmate before, always an older woman—student teacher or movie star, someone safely out of her grasp recalling in the sixth grade a crush she had on a student teacher from a local college who taught her class for half the year. That half-year left her tortured and in pain every day, with unexplained raging hormones as her gaze would travel to her teacher's shapely stocking-clad legs and tight-fitting skirt. Her throat would dry out and her tongue would stick to the roof of her mouth whenever she was called on for an answer. She couldn't bear seeing her student teacher, just as she couldn't bear not seeing her. She didn't know what she would have done if any of those older women would've acted on her feelings. *It probably would have scared me shitless*, she thought. Being close to those women and especially being noticed and hearing them say something nice to her was sheer ecstasy as she memorized every word they spoke, and later alone in her bedroom she'd go over the conversation in her mind again and again as her fantasies about them played out.

Now everything was changing. Katie was her own age and a classmate, and Callie couldn't run from her even if she wanted to. She practiced repeatedly in her mind what she would do if she sensed that Katie might harbor the same feelings about girls that she did. Even though she knew it was too much to hope for, it comforted her to pretend that Katie did indeed harbor those same feelings. As cool and calm as her mind portrayed her imaginary confrontation with Katie, Callie knew that probably wouldn't be the case in reality. Katie already made her turn to gelatin when she was near, and especially when she smiled at her.

Her thoughts took her back to memories of Jill and how she'd felt at the tender age of twelve when Jill had French kissed her. Her heart had accelerated at such a dizzying speed she believed it would explode right out of her chest. She hadn't wanted Jill to ever remove her lips from her own. When she did, the kiss had left her speechless. *If this wasn't normal and natural, then why did it feel so normal and natural to her?* she wondered. Everything fell into place when Jill's lips were on hers making her feel that she now knew her place in the world.

Her mother's warning echoed over and over in her mind when she'd found out about the necking Jill and she were doing. Callie tried to explain to her mother the love she felt for Jill, but being raised a strict Catholic, her mother heatedly pointed out to her how immoral she was to desire another girl. "God made our bodies different from men for a reason," she said, "to reproduce. It's not normal for two girls or two boys to be together in the same way that God intended a man and woman to be." No matter what her mother preached, though, it still didn't answer her basic question: Why the hell did she feel this way and what could she do about it? The Church preached that all were made in God's image and that God never made a mistake. Was she an exception to His rule? She certainly didn't ask to be born with these feelings, but since she had been, she needed someone to help her, because she sure as hell couldn't help herself.

Her feelings isolated her even further from her family, and they treated her as if she had a disease that they were afraid of catching, even though she was sure that her mother was the only one who knew about Jill. Callie sincerely doubted her mother would ever tell or want anyone to know that one of her children had strayed from the norm because it would be a bad reflection on her and she may be accused as the reason for the defect. That was the rationale in town whenever something went wrong in a family. Families kept the mental illnesses hushed up lest anyone think it ran in the family. Unfortunately Callie heard enough quiet whispers to know that being attracted to the same sex put one in the category of having a mental illness, and that the person in question needed to be kept away from decent society lest they infect others. Through their ignorance, they believed that homosexuality was an infectious disease, if it was indeed a disease at all. Callie didn't even understand what homosexuality was and she certainly didn't feel ill, either mentally or physically.

She had sent for some pamphlets through the mail, assured they'd arrive in a plain brown envelope and when they had, she sneaked them out of the envelope, reading the words carefully. She felt a kindred spirit with the men and women, all loving the same sex, who had written their stories and shared them openly to help those struggling with their own sexual identity. Still she tried to fight what deep down inside she already knew she was. It wasn't going to go away, and she was never going to love a man the way a woman was brought up to and it frightened her.

She sought logical causes for her difference but came up empty. She observed her older brothers, noting how they seemed perfectly contented with their girlfriends, and even Lorraine seemed happy with her husband, but Callie wasn't happy with her boyfriends—she only pretended to be. What was missing she could only get from another girl, but by dating boys, her mother stayed off her back and seemed to believe that Callie may be normal after all.

Callie thought that after Jill maybe she would finally begin to feel about boys the way everyone said a girl was supposed to. She willed herself to be aroused by boys, but it still didn't happen, only leaving her with an empty void inside. Her mother repeatedly warned her that if anyone found out what she'd done with Jill or if it happened with another girl, she'd be institutionalized. Or she'd talk to her grandmother, whom Callie held in the highest esteem, or she'd have her sent to a convent. Her mother never ceased telling her that she thought Callie's strange attraction to girls was a mental deficiency. If she did have any mental problems Callie doubted it had anything to do with liking girls, but everything to do with being mistreated and abused by a cold, uncaring family who refused to recognize the person she was inside. Just the same, she had to keep her secret locked tightly inside, never sharing it with another soul unless she was fortunate enough to meet someone like herself like when she had been fortunate enough to meet Jill.

She mused what may have been if no one had ever found out and Jill had continued her summer visits. She'd never let her mother find out that she still harbored the desire to be with girls and not boys and that her emotions were growing stronger with each passing day. Her mother kept a cautious eye on her, making certain she was well acquainted with all of her friends—Callie had grown up with most of them, so they were considered safe. But whenever she brought someone new home, she'd see her mother's stare on them, carefully weighing out the situation as she inwardly dissected the new friend and drew her own conclusions. It didn't matter to Callie since she'd never been attracted to any of them in a sexual way. She sighed. Even if she hadn't been sexually attracted to Katie, she still wanted Katie's friendship and hoped that Katie wanted hers in return. She was so unlike anyone Callie had ever known.

The weekend passed slowly and uneventfully, with Michelle calling on Sunday and acting like nothing had happened on Friday, just as Callie knew she would. They walked around Main Street, then met up with a group of friends as they enjoyed the beautiful spring day. Later they stopped at the diner for Cokes, and Callie kept her eyes peeled for any trace of Katie. She wondered if Katie had decided to get out and explore the town on her own. It would be nice to see her. She hadn't heard from her all weekend, causing a pronounced sadness within her heart that baffled her. She didn't know why she'd expected Katie to call, and rationalized the same way she had on Friday night that she should be the one to extend the invitation since Katie was new in town, but the thought of actually picking up the telephone and calling her terrified her.

She had to focus on something else, anything but Katie Johnson. Katie was messing up her mind, even though it wasn't her fault and she wasn't even aware of the affect she had on Callie. She surmised that Katie had probably met someone in her neighborhood who was showing her around. She wanted to ask Michelle if she'd seen Katie around her area but thought better of it. Callie wanted Katie to make some friends, but she wanted a special place of her own in Katie's life. She recognized the fact that she was taking this obsession about Katie to a dangerous level, but she seemed to have no control over it. She tried to convince herself that Katie was probably straight, and just being near her would have to be enough. She was willing to make that sacrifice if she had to.

Callie sighed wistfully, waiting for the day to come when hopefully she would find girls just like her who understood what she was going through and what she needed to feel whole, but until then her fantasies would have to keep her satisfied, and she'd have to keep them under control no matter how difficult it was to do at times.

Michelle plopped down in the booth. "I thought you'd dumped us this weekend for your new friend."

Callie frowned noticing that Michelle had never mentioned Katie all afternoon until they were now in Debbie's company. "Why would I?"

She shrugged. "I don't know. The way you were acting Friday."

"Hey, I was just trying to be friendly to a new classmate. That's all." She was growing tired of explaining herself.

"Well, I don't…"Michelle began.

Callie gave her a sharp look. "Just drop it, okay?"

"Touchy aren't we?" Debbie sneered.

"I don't want to deal with this shit right now," she said firmly.

"Fine," Michelle stiffly replied.

Debbie spread her hands on the table. "Okay, no more talk about your hillbilly friend."

"You're ignorant," Callie snapped.

Michelle and Debbie looked at one another and burst into laughter.

Callie held her temper. If she defended Katie too much, they would only razz her more. She bit her bottom lip as she fought to keep her turbulent emotions in check.

Chapter 4

Katie stood at her window, peering out into the dark sky illuminated by a half moon and several twinkling stars. She was lonely. She wished her mother could have found a job with set hours and preferably during the day, but her shifts were arranged throughout the twenty-four hour slot, and usually she was given second shift or the graveyard shift since she was the new waitress.

She glanced at the slip of paper gripped in her hand and squinted as she read and reread the note. All weekend long she'd fought a battle with herself about calling Callie Stone. In the end, though, she'd decided against making the call, assuring herself that Callie had probably only extended a helping hand to her on Friday because no one else had, but didn't really expect Katie to take her up on her offer to show her around town. Besides, it was evident that Callie's friends would never accept her into their circle. She looked around her barren bedroom. Her economic standing in the community upset her. She was poor, there was no denying it, and as much as she loved her mother and knew that her mother provided as best she could for her, Katie was ashamed but would never let her mother know. She didn't want anyone to find out where she lived, especially Callie Stone.

Callie made her laugh, and laughter was an emotion that had been missing from her life for too long. It felt good to forget about everything if even for a little while. She'd never fit in at school;

that was evident after the way she was stared and gawked at all day. She was embarrassed with her clothes and with herself in general, but she'd never give anyone here the satisfaction of seeing her susceptible side. She needed to be tough in this town; if she wasn't then she'd never survive.

She liked talking to Callie, and had hoped all weekend long that Callie might call her and invite her to do something. It seemed only right, since she was the new girl in town, that Callie would make the call; that was the reason she'd given her phone number to her. However, when the phone remained silent all weekend long it caused an unexplainable sadness within her. She thought about the time she'd spent with Callie on Friday, and it brought a smile to her lips. A loner by nature, Callie ignited a spark of adventure within her.

Katie turned when she heard a soft tapping on her door. "Katie, it's me, honey."

She opened the door. "Hi, Mom. I'm glad you're home. How'd work go?"

"I'm exhausted. I'm going to take a long bubble bath and finish the novel I've been reading."

Katie gave her a hug. "I'll give you a back massage when you're finished with your bath."

"I'd love that. You're such a sweet daughter." She affectionately patted her cheek. "I know you're lonely, honey, but I'm sure you'll make some friends soon."

She sighed. "I met a girl named Callie on Friday. She seems nice."

She smiled. "You should have asked her to do something this weekend."

Katie shrugged. "I suppose. We exchanged phone numbers, and I thought she'd call me. After all, I'm the new one in school."

Her mother hugged her. "Maybe she's shy, or didn't know for sure if you wanted to be friends. Sometimes you have to make the first move, Katie, if you want something bad enough. Let her know you'd like to be friends with her."

Katie's eyes twinkled. "I do want to be friends with her. She's not like the other kids around here. She's really friendly and she makes me laugh."

"Then talk to her in school tomorrow and see what happens. You have nothing to lose."

She grinned. "I will. Thanks, Mom, you always know how to make me feel better."

***

On Monday morning Callie was actually glad to go back to school, which was a drastic switch for her. The truth was that she couldn't wait to see Katie again, even if it was just to watch her in class or see her in the hall; anything was better than not seeing her at all. She rushed to her locker, grabbed her little bottle of whiskey, and after quickly surveying her surroundings, took a long swallow, then shoved the bottle back in its customary spot.

As she removed her hand, she sensed someone next to her and quickly shut her locker. Fear clutched her chest. She inhaled deeply, then slowly turned and stood face to face with Katie. Her knees buckled, but she swiftly composed herself as her gaze swept over Katie who was wearing a simple A-line skirt with a short-sleeved white blouse. The skirt was shorter than the jumper had been. She wasn't wearing socks, but because of her smooth, tanned legs Callie couldn't tell if she was wearing stockings or not. The same black flats adorned her feet.

"Hi, Callie," she said shyly.

"Hi, Katie," she replied, then realized she'd been staring at her.

"Yeah," she said self-consciously looking down at her clothes. "I guess I wasn't dressed quite right on Friday. I'm not used to the weather changes around here."

"You were fine," Callie said, hoping to ease her mind. "You're about my size. If you ever want to borrow anything, feel free. It'd be fun to borrow each other's clothes."

"Thanks."

Katie's eyes were focused on Callie's skirt. Callie suspected she was probably thinking it was too short, but she loved mini skirts, and because her figure wasn't too bad either she

could get away with wearing minis. With Katie's almost model perfect figure she'd look gorgeous in a mini skirt herself. She studied Katie's face, loving the cute way her freckles, which lightly dotted her nose, looked when she frowned. Callie was Italian and Irish, but the Irish was prominent in her features. Katie looked one hundred percent Irish.

"Did you have a good weekend? I thought maybe I'd see you around town somewhere."

"I stayed home."

"The whole weekend was nice weather. We don't get a lot of perfect weather days like this around here, so you'd better take advantage of it," she said with a grin. "Wait till next winter, then you'll know what I mean."

Katie flashed the smile she loved, and it went straight to her heart.

"So why didn't you call? We could've gotten together. I would have showed you some places to hike. Or we could have just walked or rode bikes. Hey, I still have my trusty Schwinn."

She laughed. "I didn't want to bother you. You had plans with your friends."

"You wouldn't have bothered me. I always have time for my friends, especially new ones." She knew that she owed Katie an explanation of why she hadn't called her, but at least she'd let her know in a subtle way that she considered her a friend. "If I'd known you weren't doing anything, I would have called. I just thought that you and your Mom might be busy with getting settled and everything." It was a feeble explanation, but it was the only thing she could think of.

She nodded. "That's okay. I just wanted to thank you again for helping me out on Friday."

Callie didn't want her to leave. She had to think of a reason to keep her there. "No problem. You got your schedule figured out for today?"

She raised her eyes. "I hope so. Isn't it the same as Friday?"

Callie cocked an eyebrow. "Not necessarily. When we have an assembly or a couple of days off, sometimes missed classes get added in. They shorten all the classes and then add one or two," she explained.

Katie looked confused. "I'll never figure it out."

Callie laughed. "Yes, you will. By next September you'll be a pro." She looked over Katie's schedule. "Just remember Mondays and Wednesdays are always the same, and so are Tuesdays and Thursdays. Friday has extra classes and special assemblies and all that crap. Sometimes homeroom is shorter on Fridays, too." Katie's eyes clouded doubtfully. "Don't worry about it. I still get screwed up sometimes, especially after long weekends like when we have Monday off. Then on Tuesday I'm going to Monday's classes." She shook her head.

Katie chuckled. "Yeah, that's what I'll probably end up doing, too."

Callie relaxed. "Okay, let's see." She studied Katie's schedule for a few minutes. "Cool."

"What?"

"We have three classes together starting with first period. Why don't you just hang out with me and we'll go to first class together?"

"Okay."

Michelle and Debbie headed their way. Katie apprehensively watched them approach. "What about them? I don't think they want me around, and I don't want to cause trouble between you and them."

Callie wearily sighed. "I'm sorry about them, Katie, but they'll knock it off once they get to know you."

"It's hard coming to a new school. But it's worse not fitting in."

Callie saw the sadness in her eyes and heard it in her voice.

"Sounds like me," she said, knowing that Katie didn't comprehend what she was referring to. She didn't offer a clarification to her comment, and Katie didn't ask for one. "They're so immature sometimes. They think they're being cool, but they're just making asses of themselves. Stay here and don't let them get to you. Okay?"

"Okay," she said uneasily.

Michelle ran up to her and grabbed her arm. "Come on, Cal, get a move on or we won't have time for a smoke before class."

Callie rolled her eyes. "Michelle, you say the same thing every day."

"Yeah, but you know what's gonna happen if we're late for class."

She squinted. "What do we have...maybe four or five weeks left? We're just reviewing for finals. It's no big deal."

"To some of us it is," she snapped.

Callie glanced at Katie. She looked uncomfortable, and Callie figured she probably felt left out with the chattering, so she drew her into the conversation. "Debbie, Michelle, you remember Katie?"

"Hi," Katie said brightly, looking at the both of them with a friendly smile. "It's nice to see you both."

Michelle nodded but said nothing, and Debbie looked past her like she wasn't even there. But the worst was the look that passed between Michelle and Debbie, and the smirks on their lips.

Callie's eyes flashed. She stole a look in Katie's direction. Their combined snub and the effect it had on Katie was written all over her face, with the hurt expression now evident. "Come on, Katie."

"Where're you going?" Michelle asked surprised.

"We're going to the girls' room. You'd better hurry before the bell rings," she sarcastically replied. "You wouldn't want to be late for class."

"What's the deal?"

"I asked Katie to come with us this morning."

"Hey...look, Callie...uh...Callie, I just think I'll find the class," Katie stuttered as she started down the hall.

Daggers flashed in Callie's eyes as she glared at Michelle and Debbie. She was furious. "You coming or not?"

"We'll think about it," Michelle said with a sideways glance at Debbie.

"Wait up, Katie."

Katie turned and smiled at her then they walked slowly down the corridor. Callie turned once, seeing Michelle and Debbie lagging behind them, but they were only seconds behind them as they entered the girls' room. The usual early morning chatter between them was non-existent this morning. Callie knew Katie was tense, so she thought it best not to engage her in too much conversation, especially after she'd been rebuffed, but the icy silence was killing her. She had to give it one more shot. Her friends had to see how immature and rude they were being. It wasn't Katie's fault she was an outsider, and eventually she'd fit in with the crowd if they'd just give her a chance. It'd just take some time for them to get to know her.

"Katie's in our math class, Michelle, so she's gonna walk with us to first period. She has English and history with us, too." Callie hoped this information would ease some of the tension. She lit a cigarette, took a long drag on it, and then handed it to Katie.

"Are you two in all the same classes?" Katie asked with a nod in Michelle's direction. She inhaled deeply then passed the cigarette to Michelle.

Michelle quickly lit one of her own cigarettes; Katie kept her cool as Callie bit her bottom lip to keep from exploding. Katie next offered the cigarette to Debbie, but she silently shook her head no then walked over to where Terry Brace was animatedly talking to some classmates.

"It worked out that way this year," Michelle answered, slowly exhaling. "Of course Miss Brain here," she continued with a shot in Callie's direction, "will be in all the advanced classes when we hit ninth grade. We won't be in any classes together unless I change to business courses."

"Yeah, like I'm that smart," Callie grinned, glancing at Katie.

Katie took another drag, then handed the cigarette back to Callie. "I doubt I'll be in any of those classes. I'll be lucky just to make it through general classes." She chuckled.

Michelle opened her mouth but caught Callie's eye. Whatever she was about to say, she kept to herself. "I'm outta here." Callie grabbed her purse and books. "Let's go, Katie."

"Why? First bell hasn't rung yet," Michelle said with a look of surprise on her face. "You're usually a lagger and we have to drag your butt outta here."

"I just want to make sure that Katie gets a good seat in class."

"Why? Rinehart doesn't assign seats."

"I know, so we'll try to get seats so she can sit by us." She threw the cigarette into the toilet.

Michelle made a face. Katie turned, pretending not to see, but Callie did and knew that Katie had as well. "Catch you later in class," she said, angrily slamming her foot down on the toilet handle.

＊＊＊

The rest of the week passed much too quickly, and Callie embraced every minute she got to spend with Katie. Every day she'd hint to her that it was okay to call, but Katie never did. Callie debated whether she should call Katie and invite her over to her house. After all, that's what friends did, and the way things looked Callie was the only friend Katie would have for awhile. In time, though, she was certain Katie would make loads of friends, but selfishly Callie reveled in the fact that for now at least she had her to herself.

She took every opportunity to include Katie in her circle of friends. Twice that week she had lunch the same time as Katie did, and she invited her to sit at the table with her and her friends. Katie was almost ignored as the others chitchatted among themselves. The attitude of her friends deeply disturbed Callie. Katie may not have been much of a talker, but when she did speak, she showed her sense of humor and wit. Her answers were blunt and honest, and she wasn't one to beat around the bush.

Callie was rapidly reaching the point that she had to let her friends know that their behavior was unbearable, and they had no right to choose whom she hung out with. She had to be cautious, though, because if she started spending every minute with Katie—as much as she yearned to—they'd become suspicious. If she didn't have a strong desire for more than friendship with her, then she wouldn't have worried, but she had to be very careful not to become suspect, especially to Katie. Her infatuation was growing day-by-day, hour-by-hour, minute-by-minute, and second by second. She couldn't wait to be near her. She loved the way she talked, walked, and smiled. She was head over heels in love, and it scared her shitless.

***

Katie tossed and turned, waking up with the sheets soaked from her perspiration. She'd had the dream again. In the dream everything was peaceful and quiet, and she was lying next to Callie in a field of beautiful flowers. Callie's face showed her happiness as they lay facing one another, their hands entwined.

Katie exhaled in a rush as she glanced at her alarm clock. In two hours she had to get up for school. She didn't mind school as long as she got to see Callie. That was all she looked forward to every day. She'd sit every night before bed willing the phone to ring, but night after night it remained silent. She wanted Callie to call, but she never did.

Even though she and Callie seemed to hit it off in school, she wished Callie would invite her to do something outside of school.

Callie had suggested several times that she should call if she needed anything or wanted to hang out, but Callie could never know what she truly wanted.

She closely watched Callie in class, stealing quick glances at her when she thought Callie wasn't looking. She yearned for her. Callie made her feel like she belonged and was somebody, but she saw the sadness in her eyes even though Callie tried to hide her pain with her quick wit and humor. She knew the first minute her eyes met Callie's that they had clicked and connected on a different level. There was something special about Callie Stone.

Chapter 5

The school year was rapidly coming to an end. Every morning Katie continued showing up at Callie's locker, and Callie enjoyed discussing summer plans with her. Callie had secured a summer job working at the State Park; Katie would be working for the school. She'd tried to get Katie a job in the park with her since Katie loved the outdoors so much, and selfishly because then Callie would be able to see her everyday, but all the positions were filled. Applications for summer employment had to be filed by the end of April, but an exception had been made in Katie's case since she'd moved to Littledale too late to make the deadline. The only job available was putting new covers on the worn books in the elementary school.

Callie hoped she'd see Katie over the summer knowing she couldn't bear to lose the bright spark Katie had brought into her otherwise mundane life. She never missed one opportunity to be in Katie's presence, and she knew she'd sorely feel the void when the school year finished. Katie hadn't made many friends, even though people outside of Callie's own group of friends were beginning to warm to her. She seemed to hold herself back from people and didn't seem interested in forging close friendships. Callie was coming to the conclusion that Katie was a loner and didn't care much for socializing, but all and all Katie showing up at her locker each morning was the highlight of her day. Sometimes Katie would wait after school with her until Callie's second trip bus came. They'd smoke a cigarette and talk. Callie waited for

Katie to mention them getting together outside of school, but she never did.

Callie had finally decided to invite her to spend the night the last weekend of school. If she didn't extend the invitation, then the summer would be long and lonely without seeing her. Callie suspected the reason Katie wouldn't invite her over was because she lived in The Projects. Actually, the Projects were very nice apartments with well-kept grounds, but they had a stigma attached to them. It was common knowledge that the inhabitants were low-income or—as became aptly known—the working poor. Katie had said that her family only consisted of she and her mother, and as hard as her mother worked, Callie doubted she made a fortune waitressing. Callie didn't tell Katie that she knew where she lived, instead hoped that if she accepted her invitation to spend the night she might return the invitation, and then she would see that it didn't matter to Callie where she lived. Callie wanted to continue building their budding friendship and not let it languish for two months.

She was worried about asking Katie over though, knowing that her huge family could be overwhelming to someone who wasn't used to the every day commotion of a large family, but she had to make a move since Katie wasn't going to. It was now or never.

On Friday morning she waited at her locker for Katie. Katie greeted her with her usual smile.

"Morning, Cal."

Callie returned her smile. "Hi, Katie. Do you have any plans for tomorrow?"

She raised her eyebrows. "No."

"Want to come over to my house? You can spend the night if you want to."

"Okay," she replied without any hesitation, surprising Callie and making Callie wish she'd invited her sooner.

"Why don't I walk to your house tomorrow to pick you up, and then we can walk back to mine? What's your address?"

"That's too much for you to walk to this end of town and then back again."

"I don't mind. I love walking."

Her eyes shifted. "I know where you live. I'll have my Mom give me a lift before she goes to work."

Callie sensed that Katie still didn't want her to know where she lived, and she had to find a way to convince her that it didn't matter. What was inside a person mattered a whole lot more than where they lived, as far as Callie was concerned. "That'd be great, then."

***

Callie could hardly wait for Saturday, and when it finally came she rushed through her weekend chores, then straightened her bedroom—not that it was messy, but she was a fanatic when it came to her room. Everything had a proper place and she diligently kept it organized. She timidly awaited Katie's arrival. She'd never been nervous before when one of her friends stayed over, but she wanted everything to be perfect for Katie. Katie wasn't just anyone. She'd mentioned to her mother that she'd met a new friend and had invited her to spend the night. Her mother nodded but kept silent, and Callie knew she'd be keeping her eyes peeled on Katie.

Katie arrived a little after four and shyly followed Callie upstairs to her room, then set her overnight bag down next to her bed. "Your house is big," she said.

Callie laughed. "With the size of my family we need the space. Is your house big?" Callie had no idea what the inside of an apartment in The Projects consisted of. Maybe now Katie would share her address with her.

She shook her head. "No, but we don't need a lot of space." She looked around the room.

Callie proudly watched her. She'd turned her bedroom almost into an apartment, and if she had cooking facilities and a bathroom, she wouldn't ever have to venture out into the world of the vultures known as her family.

"This is nice," she remarked.

"Thanks. Do you want to watch TV or listen to records? We have some time before supper."

"Okay."

Her answer as usual was short, confusing Callie so she didn't know if that meant Katie wanted TV or music so she flicked on the TV. An old John Wayne western was playing. Callie sprawled on the floor and Katie sat down on the bed. "I love westerns," she announced eyes glued to the set.

Callie smiled to herself. For some reason Katie's revelation didn't surprise her. She watched the TV, but her mind was on Katie. She couldn't believe that she was finally here and in her bedroom. She needed to find a way that would make Katie want to return.

When they went downstairs to supper, Katie's face showed her awe with the enormity of Callie's family seated around the large table. Callie barely recalled any suppertime when there weren't two or three extra places at the table for friends or unexpected visitors. That was one trait she highly commended her mother for, she was always sure to have more than enough food for the family and anyone else who may show up. Callie introduced Katie to everyone and she was politely greeted, but her nervousness was evident—at least to Callie. Katie took the chair next to her. Callie's mother actually surprised her by making pleasant conversation with Katie, asking normal questions that any mother would ask of one of her children's new friends, and Callie was relieved that her questions to Katie were only general. Her younger siblings thankfully didn't embarrass her by commenting on Katie's southern accent, but she assumed they were too eager to get back outside to play to pay much attention to anything but gulping down their food in the least amount of time as possible.

After supper, Callie gave her a tour of the rest of the house, then they went back upstairs to her room where they listened to music and smoked cigarettes. Callie hoped Katie would relax and be comfortable. Maybe outside of school she might feel less inhibited and open up more, and since this was the first time they'd actually been totally alone together Callie felt the burning need to know everything there was to know about her. "Do you smoke pot?" She hoped her question didn't alarm Katie, but she needed to know. If she were totally against it, then Callie would make sure she never mentioned it to her again.

"I've never tried it," she hesitantly answered.

"How do you feel about it?"

"I don't know…I guess it's no different that getting snoggered on alcohol."

"Do you want some?"

Katie carefully eyed her. "Not right now. Maybe later."

Callie smiled. "I won't smoke any either, then. Does it bother you that I smoke pot?"

She shook her head. "No."

Callie grabbed a couple of bottles of beer from her bureau drawer. "Do you drink?"

"Sometimes."

She handed a bottle to her. "Sorry it's a little warm. For obvious reasons I can't keep it in the fridge," she laughed.

Katie took the beer and opened it. "How do you get this stuff?" She peered at the assortment of bottles of wine and whiskey in Callie's bottom bureau drawer. "Doesn't your mother ever look in there?"

"No, that's one thing I give her credit for, she never snoops in our rooms or opens our mail. Someday I'll probably find a better hiding place, 'cause I don't trust my brothers and sisters."

"So how do you get all this?"

Callie cocked an eyebrow. "I have my ways."

Katie didn't respond.

"No, actually the guy at the liquor store thinks my Mom is a drunk, 'cause my brothers turned me on to going there and saying it was for her. Everybody in town knows that she doesn't get out much because of her leg—she had polio—and since she's a widow with ten kids they probably feel sorry for her and assume she needs to imbibe to keep her sanity. Most of the beer, though, I get at Brawns Market. We pay for our groceries once a month, so I just stick the extra money in or I don't give her the slip. Usually she's too busy to go over all the slips anyway." She opened her beer and took a long swallow. "Do you want some whiskey or wine?"

"Maybe later."

Callie nodded to her wide assortment of forty-fives and albums. "Pick out what records you want to hear. I have just about everything." Her passion for music showed in the hundreds of forty-fives and albums neatly stacked in cases.

She loved having Katie sitting in her room looking at her things, and she noticed that Katie started to loosen up. At first Callie thought it was the beer, but she'd only had a few sips. *So it must be me*, she inwardly rejoiced. "So, Katie, do you have any big plans for summer other than working?"

Katie handed her an album and she put it on the stereo. "Not really." She leafed through one of the numerous scrapbooks Callie kept of her favorite movie stars.

"Well, at least you're making friends now, so it won't be so lonely for you."

She shrugged. "They're okay, but I'm used to being by myself a lot. I don't mind being alone."

"Don't you like being around people?"

She looked at Callie. "Yeah, I like people, but it's hard to find someone who likes the same things I do. Most of the girls in school are only interested in chasing boys."

"I know," she agreed with a nod.

"You have a boyfriend."

"Yeah, but he lives in Pennsylvania. I don't see him too much."

She frowned. "Doesn't that bother you? I mean if you care

about someone, don't you want to spend as much time as you can together?"

She tossed her head. "He has his own life and I have mine. I have other stuff I like to do, too, things he has no interest in."

"Is that why you hardly talk about him unless Michelle or Debbie ask you something?"

"I suppose."

"I can't stand how most of the girls in school act around their boyfriends—stupid, and like they don't have a mind of their own. When they aren't with their boyfriends, they talk only about them and act like they don't have a life without them. And the ones who don't have a steady boyfriend only talk about the boys they have a crush on. Talking about boys all of the time is the only conversation they want to have. Know what I mean? But you're not like them."

Callie took her last remark as a compliment. "Yeah, they're clones of their mothers around here. Find a good man, get married, and have a bunch of squawking brats." She laughed as she finished her beer. "I could never be like them. There's too much living to do." Her eyes grew wide. "Like I told you before, I like writing, being with my friends, and sometimes just being by myself. I have more important things to do then to spend all my time and energy chasing after boys, and that's why Jack and I have a perfect relationship. I like him more the less I see of him."

Katie chuckled.

Callie noticed Katie's perfectly clear skin. She didn't have one blemish or even the hint of one. *Must be nice*, she thought, painfully aware that she never knew when she'd awaken to find a horrifying pimple dotting her face and consequently ruining her whole day, especially when it happened on a day like school pictures or something important. "Why don't you ever date? I know a couple of boys who like you. I heard them talking in math class about you."

She blushed. "Nah, I'm too much of a tomboy. I haven't reached the stage yet where I'm interested in boys that way."

Her answer didn't tell Callie much. "I like hanging out with boys sometimes. They can be a lot of fun as friends if they don't try for something I don't want to give them."

When Katie made no response Callie dropped the subject, and they returned to discussing their favorite singers and movie stars, and what movies they'd seen and wanted to see.

Later, as they prepared for bed, Callie watched Katie slip her shirt over her head, revealing her lean smooth shoulders. Then she unhooked her bra, letting loose two beautifully formed breasts. Her breasts were bigger than Callie's, and Callie didn't know why that fact surprised her, but strangely, it did. From the way Katie clothed herself it had been difficult for Callie to get a picture of what type of breasts she really had. Callie's gaze stayed riveted on Katie, watching her remove her jeans and beholding her legs, those long, strong and perfectly shaped legs. Katie was now only clad in her underwear, and the sight of her almost naked body made Callie's breath momentarily catch in her throat. Her cheeks flamed, forcing her to quickly turn away before Katie saw the yearning in her eyes. With her back to Katie, Callie quickly removed her own clothes, then threw a nightgown over her head.

"What side do you want to sleep on?" she asked, hoping to keep her voice steady.

"It doesn't matter. Sleep on the side you usually do," she answered with a bright smile. "After all, it's your bed."

"If I get up in the night, don't worry. I have a back problem, and sometimes if it aches too much I sleep on the floor. It seems to help."

Her eyes filled with concern. "That's too bad. Did you have an accident?"

"No, it's been this way for years. I'm used to it. I've been taking pain killers for a while now." She climbed into her twin-sized bed. The size of her bed had never bothered her before when any of her other friends stayed over, but with Katie here now, it did bother her because having her so close all through the night, knowing the feelings she secretly harbored about her, overwhelmed Callie.

She moved to the outside of the bed and Katie lay by the wall. Then she turned out the light and they chatted for a while, giggling over Callie's silly jokes.

An hour later Callie heard her soft even breathing, and in her sleep Katie's bare leg touched hers, sending shivers down Callie's spine. She was afraid of her lack of self-control and moving too closely, and touching her if she stayed in the bed any longer. She grabbed her pillow and quietly slipped out of bed to lie on the floor. Minutes later she heard Katie stir, the bed creaked, and Katie was kneeling over her.

"Cal, does your back hurt?" she whispered.

"Not too much. I'm sorry I woke you. Please go back to sleep."

"It's okay. I'll give you a massage if you want me to. Sometimes I massage my Mom's back."

"You don't have to do that. It's late, and you're probably tired." Callie's heart was thumping so loudly she was certain that Katie could hear it.

"No, really, I'd like to," she insisted. "I hate to see anyone suffering."

She took a nervous breath. "Okay, what do I do?"

"Take your nightgown off or you can leave it on if you want, but it works better on bare flesh," she replied. "Just lie there on your stomach."

She removed her nightgown and pulled a sheet over her legs and buttocks. She inhaled sharply, feeling Katie's tender hands on her back. A tremor tore through her as Katie skillfully kneaded her flesh. She was grateful that the darkness shrouded her face.

"How does that feel?" Katie quietly asked.

Callie felt her warm breath close to her ear. "Real good," she murmured. "I never had a massage before. Guess I'll have to keep you around."

"I don't mind. Just call me whenever you need one."

Callie closed her eyes as Katie's hands moved over her entire back. She sucked in her breath as those intense hands continued touching her throbbing body longing to turn over and pull Katie down on top of her but knew she couldn't do that. When Katie was finished, Callie could still feel the sensation from her touch, and couldn't recall ever feeling so relaxed and peaceful.

"I hope that helped."

"It did. Thanks, Katie. I'm going to stay here for a while." She sighed contentedly as Katie climbed back into bed. Callie stayed on the floor the rest of the night, drifting in and out of sleep as she relived the feel of those hands on her body and shivered at the wanton emotions they'd brought out in her. She swallowed hard as she ached for a love she couldn't have and was too frightened to seek.

***

Katie bit her bottom lip. She had wanted to put her lips on Callie's back and neck and shower her with tender kisses, but the closest she could get to her was massaging her naked back. She could have massaged her forever and never grown tired of stroking her.

Callie confused her, but at least she'd found out that she wasn't serious about her boyfriend Jack. That gave her comfort. She lay in the dark in Callie's bed, the bed Callie slept in every night, totally aware of Callie's presence. She willed Callie to climb back into bed next to her. She quietly let her breath out, closing her eyes as her mind pictured how it would feel to hold Callie in her arms.

***

When Callie awoke in the morning Katie was already dressed and standing by the window smoking a cigarette. She propped herself up on an elbow. "Early riser?"

She grinned. "Yeah, that's me. Up with the chickens, as my Mom says."

Callie yawned, then stretched. "You have a good relationship with your mother, don't you?"

"Yeah, she's more like my best friend at times. We've always been close"

"She sounds cool. Maybe I can meet her some time."

"Yeah, she is."

She noticed that Katie ignored any comment about Callie meeting her mother. "So do you have any special time you have to get home today?"

She shook her head.

"Good. How about we go for a walk? I can show you some great places to hike."

Her eyes lit up. "I'd like that."

***

They spent the day walking around town as Callie pointed out all the teenage hangouts to Katie. Their conversation finally turned to their mutual love of running, and they decided to have a race on the high school track. Katie was an excellent runner and was the first girl Callie ever knew who could outrun her, but it didn't upset her. Usually Callie was in competition even if it was a contest of her own making with other girls she'd raced, but with Katie she didn't feel competitive. Katie showed her how to better pace herself and conserve her strength for when it would best serve her. They raced a few times and Callie lost each race, but Katie patiently explained her weaknesses to her, demonstrating techniques and exercises Callie could use to strengthen her upper arms and legs. Callie found herself amazed at Katie's vast knowledge of running and hung onto every word she spoke.

"I haven't run like this in a long time. This is fun."

Katie smiled. "Yeah, girls our age seem to think they have to stop doing fun things unless they're trying for the Olympics or are on a school team. God forbid they should still ride a bike."

Callie grinned. "I know. I asked Michelle this spring to go

bike riding with me and she looked at me like I was nuts. It's like when you get into junior high you're supposed to instantly not like all the things you really do like."

"Yeah. I don't know why people just don't do the things they like to do without worrying all the time about what everyone thinks. It's stupid."

"Well, whenever you want to go bike riding I'll go with you."

"That'd be fun. We'll have a race," she said with a sly grin. "I'll see how good you really are."

"You're on," Callie said. "Do you want to come back to my house, or do you want to go home from here since we're so close to where you live?"

"I'd like to go back to your house for a while, if it's okay with you."

"That'd be great," Callie grinned.

She wanted to walk her home that evening, but Katie adamantly refused, and Callie knew it was because she still didn't want her to know where she lived. She didn't press the issue, but hoped that Katie would eventually offer her an invitation to visit her home.

Callie lay in her bed that night with her hands behind her head, staring up at the ceiling. Her heart pounded as her thoughts took her back to the previous night. She touched the spot where Katie had lain; still smelling her fresh scent, and a smile crossed her lips.

Chapter 6

School had been out for two weeks, it was the end of the first full week at her summer job, and Callie hadn't heard from Katie since they'd said goodbye on the last day of school. She missed their daily conversations and thought they'd continue outside of school. They'd had so much fun the weekend Katie had stayed over, and Callie knew Katie had enjoyed herself that weekend, but Katie hadn't mentioned getting together again. Callie wondered if she'd offended her in some way, but nothing came to mind and Katie seemed all right the final days of school.

***

Katie sat on the sofa with her face propped in her hands. "I hate my job."

Bobbi Johnson looked up from her needlepoint. "Honey, you don't have to work if you don't want to. It was your decision."

She sighed. "No, Mom, we need the money. Besides, what would I do all summer?"

"Why don't you invite one of the girls you work with over some afternoon or give Callie a call? You need to get out of this apartment once in a while and have some fun with girls your own age."

She made a face. "They're all snobs around here—except

for Callie. I wish I could've gotten a job in the park. At least I wouldn't be cooped up in a crummy hot school all day long."

"Doesn't Callie work in the park?"

She nodded.

"Why don't you give her a call and ask her to do something?"

"Why doesn't she call me?"

Bobbi slowly let her breath out. "Are you and Callie fighting?"

She shook her head.

"You said you had a good time the weekend you stayed at her house."

"I did."

"Then what's the problem?"

"I don't know."

"Well, Callie made the first move by inviting you over."

"I don't know…I'm just mixed up."

Bobbi eyed her carefully. "Honey, are you having different feelings for Callie?"

Katie's face turned crimson.

"When you told me that you were attracted to girls, I told you it would be difficult, especially if you aren't sure the girl you like has those same kind of feelings for you."

Katie sighed. "That's my problem. I don't know how to find out."

"Suppose you do find out and what if Callie isn't the way you hope she'll be? Will you still be able to be just friends with her?"

"I think so, but sometimes I think she is and then she'll say something and it makes me think I only imagined it just because it's what I want."

Bobbi's eyes narrowed. "Just be careful, honey. There's the chance that if Callie finds out about you she may not want to associate with you."

"Yeah, I know. I thought about that, too."

"Well, she obviously likes you or she wouldn't have spent so much time with you in school. I think you need to make the next move if you want to be friends with her. She may be hurt that you didn't return the invitation to have her stay over here some night. Why don't you call her and ask her to get together?" She set her needlepoint down. "I know you're having a difficult time, honey, with the move and everything."

"I'll be okay. It's been a long, tiring day. It's boring putting covers on books all day long."

Bobbi laughed. "I suppose it is, Katie."

She stood up. "I'm going to take a shower, and then maybe I'll give Callie a call."

***

Callie spent the first week of vacation hanging out with Michelle, Linda, and Terry, going to the movies and roaming around town in search of a summer adventure. She was the only one of the group who was working for the summer. Dana had a job in the Administration Building in the park, but Callie didn't get to see her because she worked outside picking up trash. They rode the bus, where they got a chance to chat, to and from work, but Dana's conversations usually consisted of her new boyfriend so Callie knew she wouldn't be seeing too much of her over the summer.

She was thankful for her job not only for the money it provided, but also for helping to occupy her thoughts, which were usually centered on Katie. She felt the void in her life already and it saddened her. She missed seeing Katie every day. She was fighting the pangs of love, and if it was with a boy there would have been no problem, but how could she possibly tell Katie that she was hopelessly in love with her and it was eating away at her insides? She kept her feelings locked deep within her heart and put on a false front to her friends and family, but her diary knew the true depths of her feelings.

***

Callie was surprised a week later, on a Friday afternoon, to find a message from Katie waiting for her when she got home from work. A smile broke across her face as she quickly dialed Katie's number, hoping everything was all right. Katie picked up on the second ring.

"Hi, Katie, its Cal...What's up?" she said, controlling the trembling in her voice.

"Hi, Cal, I wanted to ask you if you're busy this weekend. I...I thought maybe we could do something," she shyly suggested. "I know its last minute."

Katie's voice was like music to her ears, but her words were what captivated her. Katie wanted to see her. Callie smiled. "Sure. When?"

"Do you want to go running or for a bike ride tomorrow?"

"That'd be cool."

Callie was ecstatic when she hung up the phone.

***

Katie grinned when she saw Callie pedaling as fast as she could to catch up with her. "Come on, slow poke," she teased. When Callie was almost side-by-side, she'd speed off. Finally, she turned into a park, parked her bike and plopped down on a bench.

Seconds later Callie pedaled up to her. "No fair," she panted. "But I have to admit, you are fast."

Katie laughed. "What else do you like to do?"

"I don't know if I dare say. You'll probably beat the pants off me like you do with everything else."

They jumped back on their bikes and rode side by side, making plans to do more things together. Callie thought her heart would burst, knowing that there was so much she wanted to share with Katie and hoped Katie would share with her. It would take time, but she was determined to make this the best summer either of them ever had.

That day brought them closer together, bonding and sealing their budding friendship. They began spending most of their free time together walking, running, riding bikes and talking—even though Callie did most of the talking. She was surprised one day when Katie picked up her guitar and started strumming. She had a beautiful voice and was an excellent guitar player.

"I didn't know you played."

Katie shrugged. "Just something I picked up."

Callie lay back on her bed, listening as Katie strummed a popular love ballad, then closed her eyes as Katie's voice echoed the pain of the woman in the song. Callie was mesmerized. She could sit and listen to Katie play and sing for hours and never tire of hearing her. She pretended the words Katie sang were just for her.

***

One evening they were relaxing after supper in Callie's bedroom, propped up on pillows on the floor a gentle rain falling outside, when Katie confessed how she despised her job. The girls she'd been assigned to work with were stuck-up and mostly spent the day gossiping, barely being civil to her. She was hurt at their snide remarks and the whispering behind her back. Callie felt sorry for her, knowing how fortunate she was to have the job she did. She loved everything about her job, including her co-workers, and they had a blast in the park that summer swimming and picnicking with the blessings of their supervisors. Sometimes she almost felt guilty for receiving a paycheck for having fun. She wished that she and Katie could have worked together, and she promised Katie that maybe next summer they would be able to work together if they put their applications in early and requested where they wanted to work. It was usually first come first serve, and it didn't hurt if the guidance counselor in charge of the program liked you. Callie knew him well and was fortunate that he did indeed like her. Just the same, she was infuriated that people could be so ignorant and cruel. She wished she could defend Katie, but there was nothing she could do except assure Katie that those girls were a bunch of losers anyway.

Each night Callie lay in her bed going over the conversations she and Katie had shared that day. On the days she didn't get to see Katie she would write love poems and short stories, letting her imagination explore possibilities that her conscious mind doubted would ever come to pass. Sometimes when she looked at Katie she flushed, remembering what she'd written the night before. She relished Katie's friendship and was thankful just to have her in her life, even if it was only as a friend.

Katie excelled at everything athletic, and her talents were endless. They shot hoops—one of Callie's favorite activities—went to movies, listened to music and discussed the war in Viet Nam and women's rights. Katie didn't care much for politics and looked at her with an amused expression on her face whenever Callie become enraged and would enthusiastically try to get Katie to see her point of view. Katie taught her that people were more apt to listen to what she had to say if she presented her argument in a peaceful, calm manner instead of charging in like a lunatic. What she said made sense, even though Callie didn't necessarily agree with her descriptive choice of words, but Katie was direct and Callie truly respected her honesty.

Katie loved walking in the gentle summer rains and chasing after rainbows as much as she did, and they started wishing on the first star of the night when they were together, not caring that others might think them childish. She'd never been able to share simple pleasures with any of her other friends, but now all Callie knew was that she finally felt alive and had never before experienced such a zest for life, ready to embrace each new day with open arms.

Callie tried to encourage Katie to try out for girls' basketball or some other sport, but she had no desire to be on any team dealing with the high school. Callie couldn't say that she blamed her, even though Katie would have been an asset to any team or the chorus or band. Katie had no desire to share her music with the public and seemed to enjoy playing and singing only for her own pleasure and Callie's.

Callie continued dating Jack and hanging out with the crowd, sometimes bringing Katie along, but Katie was uncomfortable around her friends. The best times Callie had that summer, though, were spent alone with Katie, but she couldn't abandon her other friends or Jack, even though she would have in a heartbeat if it wouldn't draw attention to her. Katie understood her and most importantly cared about her, but sometimes she wondered if Katie suspected her true feelings or if Katie felt the same way about her. Occasionally she caught Katie watching her with a strange look in her eyes, but she couldn't come right out and ask her. She didn't want to do anything to jeopardize their friendship and fought to keep her emotions in check around her, even though she longed to touch her for just a second.

Callie's mother was cordial to Katie, but Callie sensed that she didn't like her, making it obvious to Callie by never going out of her way to treat her like family as she did with the rest of Callie's friends. She mentioned to Callie that "that girl", as she referred to Katie, seemed to be spending a lot of time with her, infringing on Callie's long term friendships. She saw the evil eye her mother would occasionally flash at Katie when Katie was unaware. Callie knew she needed to hide her feelings about Katie from the world no matter how it made her feel like she was suffocating. She anguished when she was with Katie and anguished when they were apart. Callie had picked up a few of Katie's phrases as Katie had hers, but Mrs. Stone used that to mean that Katie was a bad influence on Callie. Callie laughed, knowing that Katie had a positive effect on her entire life. Her friendship gave to Callie something she'd never had before.

If Katie noticed Mrs. Stone's aloofness, she didn't mention it and continued to frequently spend the night. Callie noticed, though, that Katie avoided being around her house near mealtimes and avoided contact with anyone in her family as much as possible. She knew that Katie wasn't at ease around large groups of people. It bothered Katie the way Callie was treated by her own family, even though they never discussed it, but she'd see Katie's eyes momentarily flash with anger whenever Mrs. Stone unjustly reprimanded her for something Callie didn't do, but Katie kept silent. In time Callie was certain she'd question her about her home life, but no doubt, she realized why Callie spent almost every moment she was home up in her room, referring to it as her private fortress.

***

Callie looked forward to the fantastic back massages Katie gave her every time she stayed over, which was becoming more and more frequent as the summer wore on. Katie confided to her that she was worried about entering high school and laughingly said Callie would probably dump her for a more exciting crowd, but Callie assured her that it would never happen, neglecting to tell her that she couldn't dump her even if she wanted to.

They became comfortably at ease with one another with Katie sprawling on the bed watching TV or listening to music, and Callie lying on the opposite end writing or reading. Callie loved the classics, and her favorite authors were Louisa May Alcott and the Brontë sisters—Emily and Charlotte. Whenever the old movie versions of *Jane Eyre*, *Wuthering Heights*, or *Little Women* came on TV, Katie would sit and watch them with her. Callie could watch them over and over and never tire of them. George Orwell made Callie think, and she read Animal Farm a couple of times before it was even assigned. She also loved poetry, Elizabeth Barrett Browning and Emily Dickinson being her favorite poets. Katie wasn't much of a reader, and as much as Callie tried to turn her on to literature she just didn't share her passion, but she did enjoy the poetry Callie wrote and then recited to her. She was her captive audience of one, and even though Callie's poetry was usually dark and brooding, Katie didn't know that those poems with all the teenage angst were about her.

Whenever Callie received, what she jokingly referred to as, a prohibited paperback delivered through the mail in the customary brown wrapping paper, Katie's interest was piqued. She'd flip through the pages, reading the torrid love scenes aloud causing them both to double over in laughter with her rendition of the heroine's passionate lines.

For the first time in her life, Callie was almost content. She knew what it felt like to truly share all of her hopes and dreams with someone without fearing ridicule. The only gloomy side to her newfound contentment was the twice or more monthly times she had to seclude herself from everyone. Katie never questioned her mysterious absences, and as much as Callie longed to tell her why she had to go away, she couldn't. She'd been living with this horrible secret since the age of eight and she didn't know for how much longer she could endure the pain and humiliation, but she also worried about Katie's reaction if she found out. Katie never pried and Callie respected her for that. It was an unwritten courtesy they extended to one another.

Callie continued to throw out hints about visiting Katie's home, but she never came right out and asked her why she wouldn't invite her. At times Callie wondered if there was another reason besides where she lived that would explain why she never received an invitation to Katie's home.

Callie turned Katie on to pot that summer, watching gleefully as Katie let her hair down and showed another side of her personality. When Katie was high she'd giggle and chat incessantly, a total contrast to her normal self, and when something excited or agitated her she'd open her mouth to speak, but only guttural sounds would come out.

Katie normally had a healthy appetite, but marijuana made her need for food almost insatiable. One night she got a craving for pizza, and as much as Callie tried to cajole her into having something else, the yen just wouldn't leave her. Callie wouldn't have been concerned except that a violent storm had blown in, and Katie had decided to ride her bike to the pizza shop. The more Callie protested the more Katie resolved to go.

Callie was terrified of storms and Katie knew that. Callie was petrified to let her go out into the vile weather, but she couldn't stop her, especially when she was high. She stood by her bedroom window, paralyzed with fear as sharp streaks of lightning flashed, followed by ear-shattering cracks of thunder. Rain pelted so hard against the window that at times she couldn't see a thing. She silently prayed for Katie's safety, and after what seemed like an eternity she saw Katie pedaling down the parking lot like it was a beautiful, sunny day oblivious to the violent weather. She steered her bike with one hand as she balanced three large pizzas on the other, ignoring the rain pouring down on her. How she kept the pizzas and herself intact Callie would never know, but moments later Katie came into her room dripping. "I'm back," she said nonchalantly, flashing Callie a smile as bright as the lightning. Callie shook her head in wonder, then watched her ravenously dig into the pizza. They devoured the three pizzas that night.

One humid evening at the end of summer Katie turned to her with a solemn expression on her face and said, "I wish we were sisters. It's fun having you to confide in and talk to."

Callie raised her eyes. "If we were sisters we probably would be the way I am with mine—not close."

"Yeah, I've noticed. You don't seem like you fit in with your family."

She squinted. "Maybe I'm adopted. But if I could choose anyone to be my sister it would be you."

Katie's eyes twinkled. "I've got an idea."

"What?"

"You'll think it's silly," she said sheepishly.

"No, I promise. Come on, Katie, tell me."

She chewed her bottom lip. "Let's be blood sisters—that's the next closest thing to being real sisters."

Callie grinned. "Okay. I'd like that." Actually, she was excited to have her blood mixed with Katie's, even if it was just a finger prick. She held out her finger and Katie pricked it with a needle, then pricked her own.

"There, now we're sisters forever," she triumphantly announced, pinching their two fingertips together.

Callie trembled as Katie held her fingertip, knowing she'd treasure this moment for the rest of her life. "And all through eternity," she added.

"Yes," Katie said, motivated now. "We'll be soul mates in life and death. We'll always be there for each other no matter what. This is our promise to each other, and no one will ever be able to break our bond."

They sealed their union with a wine toast, clinking their wine jugs together. A soft peacefulness crept through Callie, and she so desperately wanted to share with Katie the two secrets that were haunting her soul, but she was terrified of Katie's reaction. She couldn't let anything destroy her newfound happiness; even though she was certain that Katie would understand once she explained it. But rationality still nagged at her—what if Katie couldn't or wouldn't empathize with her? They vowed never to keep secrets from one another and eventually the day would come when she would have to tell her, so she appeased herself with the fact that the proper time would present itself.

Chapter 7

The new school year began on a happy note, and even though they shared no classes together, Katie continued her ritual of meeting Callie at her locker each morning. Michelle and Debbie eventually began acknowledging Katie's presence, but their actions made it clear that she still didn't and probably never would fit in. Their dislike of Katie stemmed from jealousy because they couldn't hold a candle to her in looks and figure, and Callie sensed that they couldn't stand the fact that she seemed to enjoy Katie's company to theirs.

Being with Katie made Callie feel, for the first time in her life, that she was somebody and that she was truly cared about. Everyone, especially her family, had always made her feel like an outsider. Sure, she was good enough when it enhanced their needs, but if she needed something she was quickly brushed aside, as long as she was doing for them and not asking or expecting anything in return she was okay. No one had ever cared about the silent girl who still held the suffering child deep within her soul, and as the child grew into a young woman, the child stayed tucked safely inside, enjoying the luxury of youth when Katie brought her out to play. All Katie asked for was her friendship with no strings attached, and the rewards Callie received from her friendship vastly outweighed any friendships she'd ever before had. She truly was the kindest, most self-sacrificing person Callie would ever know, and even without the crush she had on Katie, she would still feel this way.

Now that they were in high school Callie began to associate with an older crowd, but Katie still took top priority in her life. Katie wasn't comfortable with parties, but she loved going to football games, and when Callie went to parties Katie would still show up at her house late at night when her mother was working the graveyard shift.

They were the only fourteen-year-olds in town without a curfew. It had its ups and downs, though, earning Callie a reputation for being wild, but it also gave her the insight to what people really did late at night and who was sneaking out of what house in the wee hours of the morning. As long as her chores were done and Callie wasn't getting into trouble, her mother kept quiet. She never minded Callie's friends and her drinking at home; with the only substances she had zero tolerance for being drugs. What she didn't know wouldn't hurt her, was Callie's philosophy. Once Callie tried to point out to her that the Valium she depended on to get her through each day was a drug, but her argument fell on deaf ears. Since her trusted doctor's opinion was right up there with God's and he would never prescribe something that could harm her, she closed her ears and mind to the subject, so Callie never brought the topic up again. But unbeknownst to her mother, Callie also shared her love of Valium and her mother was never the wiser.

Katie wouldn't pop pills or do anything more than smoke an occasional joint, and hinted a few times that maybe Callie should cut back, but she didn't press the issue and Callie didn't cut back. Callie needed to kill the pain of her degradation, and she knew of no other way short of ending her life. Now even that was not an option with Katie in her life.

***

One night Katie and Callie were sprawled out on Callie's bed, listening to music. Something felt different tonight, but Callie couldn't put her finger on it. She stole a glance at Katie, who had her eyes focused on one of Callie's many posters, but Callie sensed that she wasn't really looking at the poster at all. Instead, she seemed lost in her own thoughts. "Is everything okay, Katie?"

She was thoughtful for a moment. "Have you ever thought about marriage, kids and all that?" she finally asked.

Callie raised her eyebrows, surprised at Katie's unusual question. "Not really. I suppose though that's the route everybody thinks I'll eventually take, but I'm gonna surprise the hell out of 'em. I'll probably join the Navy, be a writer, you know, all those cool things…see the world and get as far away from this city as I can."

She laughed. "Yeah, I know what you mean. I can't imagine living here forever."

"What do you want to do?"

"I'm not sure."

Callie shrugged. "You're only fourteen, so you have time to decide what you want to do with your life. Who knows, things might change by then and women might finally have equal rights. Look at what the women's rights movement is doing." She got off the bed, lit several candles, and turned off the lamp, then lay back down and faced Katie. "What's wrong, Katie?"

"It would be nice just to be treated as an equal with my own sex."

Callie sighed as she looked into Katie's eyes, seeing the pain Katie tried so hard to hide. Callie knew how much it hurt her, and it made her wonder how Katie would feel if she knew how much it also hurt her to see the pain she was in, unable to put an end to it. "I wish my friends would treat you better, Katie. It bothers me."

She looked down at her hands. "You can't control what anyone else wants to think, but they don't even try to get to know me. They know nothing about me."

"I know and it pisses me off. Just remember that it's their loss, not yours. Believe me. They think they're better than everybody, but they need to take a good look in the mirror. They're nothing but a bunch of jerks."

She smiled. "Thanks."

"I know what a great person, you really are. Who cares what they think?"

Katie looked uncomfortably at her. "I'm glad I met you, Cal. It makes it not so bad living here."

Callie looked at Katie's face illuminated by the flickering candlelight. She wondered what was really bothering her. She couldn't stand to see her in such emotional pain. "You're the most down-to-earth person I've ever known in my life, Katie. You're the first person to really listen and care about what I have to say. My other friends don't really give a shit about my feelings or me and only want to talk about their own lives. I could never tell them the things I tell you."

She grinned. "You're easy to talk to, too. I feel like I've known you forever, and I hope we're friends forever."

"We will be." Callie answered with a sly wink. "We're soul mates and blood sisters, remember?" she said, holding up her finger. "Besides, we've got so much in common. The last few months I've told you more than I've told people I've known my whole life."

"It's nice to say whatever we want to each other." She looked into Callie's eyes. "Have you ever felt like you were different from everyone else?" she nervously asked. "And you didn't know why?"

"All the time. You know that. I'm different from my family."

"That's not what I mean."

"What do you mean, then?"

She let her breath out in a rush. "Everybody's always telling us how we're supposed to feel all the time, and I just don't feel that way at all."

She nodded emphatically. "Yeah, and then you're accused of being weird for not having those feelings. Just because we're fourteen we're not supposed to have problems, and I'm so sick and tired of hearing 'Wait until you grow up, then you'll know what problems really are.'"

Katie laughed. "Oh God, that's it right on."

"Being our age isn't exactly easy." She sighed. "We're either told we're too young or too old."

Katie propped her chin in her hands. "Have you ever done it?" she bluntly asked.

Her question took Callie by surprise. They'd discussed just about every topic under the sun except for sex. "Uh-uh. I know people think I have but I really haven't. I've been getting accused of doing it for a long time." She cocked an eye at Katie. "Why, did someone tell you that I was a slut or something?"

She shook her head. "No, I just wondered," she quickly replied.

Callie was disturbed by Katie's question. She wondered if that was what had been bothering her all night. She took a sip of wine, then grabbed her pack of cigarettes, pulling one out and pushing the pack towards Katie. She reached for the lighter, but before she could pick it up Katie grabbed it and lit Callie's cigarette, then her own.

"Thanks." Callie took a long pull from her cigarette.

"You're welcome." Katie smiled and blew a puff of smoke out as she looked into Callie's eyes.

Katie was looking at her with a strange expression on her face and a questioning look in her eyes. She'd never looked at her like this before. "What?" she asked. The intensity of Katie's probing eyes was making her nervous and self-conscious.

"Nothing." Katie's face flushed. "Just..."

"Just what?"

She stared at her cigarette, took a long drag and let it out slowly before answering. "Have you ever thought about what it'll be like . . . you know the first time you do it?"

She frowned. "I guess everybody thinks about it once in a while. Have you?" She carefully eyed her.

"I don't know. I guess I think things maybe . . . forbidden thoughts." Her face turned a deep shade of red.

Callie grew serious. "And what are forbidden thoughts?"

Katie avoided Callie's penetrating eyes. "I don't know. I just feel different about things than the way other girls think."

"The story of my life. You've been around here long enough to know I'm different. I live in this house with all these people around me, they don't like me, and I don't know why. I'm treated like an outsider in my own family. But hey, I survive because I know it won't be this way forever. If I thought it was, then I'd never get through it." Katie chewed her bottom lip, but kept silent. "Why don't you let me set you up with someone, Katie? We can double date. It would be so much fun."

"I don't think so," she said slowly.

"Oh, come on. Jack can bring a friend the next time he comes over."

Katie shot her a questioning look.

"What?"

"You never thought of…um…doing it with Jack?"

Callie laughed again. "Hell no. I've never thought of doing it with any guy."

"Why?"

She was thoughtful for a minute as Katie's eyes stayed glued to her face causing her to feel apprehensive. "I don't know. It's hard to explain. I like guys, but you know, as friends, not…that way." She grimaced. "Maybe I'm the strange one. I haven't met a guy yet that would make me want to do it with him. I must be slow in that area of adolescence." She hoped her feeble attempt at an explanation would satisfy Katie.

Katie smiled the crooked smile Callie loved, and even though she didn't have a clue what Katie was getting at, she enjoyed the fact that she had let Katie know in a roundabout way that she didn't want to have sex with boys. Her answer seemed to appease Katie.

Katie's expression became intense. "Do you . . . um…have you…oh never mind."

"What?" Callie asked. She had no idea what was on her mind now.

She sat up. "Uh…I dunno. I shouldn't say this. I shouldn't ask you this."

"Come on, Katie, you can ask me anything. We have no secrets."

She looked down at her hands, and then took a long drag off her cigarette. "Okay, but you gotta promise not to get mad at me."

"I promise, you can ask me anything, Katie. That's why we get along so well together. We can say anything on our minds without worrying about offending each other. Just ask me. It's not gonna shock me, believe me."

She laughed self-consciously, and then inhaled deeply. "Have you ever kissed a girl before?" She let the smoke out slowly, watching Callie's expression.

The question threw Callie off guard. The incident with Jill flashed through her mind. Could she tell Katie that? Would she understand? Did she dare tell her that? Now was probably as good a time as any to tell her about Jill, but it was a loaded question. Maybe she was upset because she had kissed a girl and had been uncomfortable with it, and just wanted to talk about her feelings. Callie couldn't tell her the effect Jill's kisses had had on her, but looking at Katie's searching eyes forced her to take the risk. "Um, yeah." Her face grew hot.

"You have?" Katie's eyes widened.

"Yeah, um, it was a couple of years ago," She laughed weakly. "We were playing spin the bottle. This girl was staying with friends of mine down the street and she…um…there weren't any boys left and everybody sort of dared us to kiss and she kissed me." She swallowed the sickening lump in her throat.

Katie leaned closer. "How did you feel?"

Her face flamed. She felt like she was on fire and would spontaneously combust at any moment. "I don't know," she weakly replied.

"Did you like it?" Katie's gaze was firmly glued on her.

Callie avoided her eyes, wishing she could lie and tell Katie that she hated it, but Katie would only see through her deception. "I don't know. I guess I didn't hate it." Her palms perspired as her heart beat faster. How would Katie feel about her now? Her lips trembled as fear gripped her chest.

Katie grew quiet. Callie needed to know what she was thinking and how she was processing this new revelation about her. After what seemed like an eternity of silence, Callie nervously looked at her. Katie stared at her with a strange, haunted look in her eyes. Everything moved in slow motion and they were suspended in time. Katie moved closer and closer to her, their eyes locked together. Before she could grasp what was happening, Katie's soft and gentle lips were on hers. A warm awareness ignited her body and she swallowed hard as the blood rushed to her head.

Katie removed her lips and backed away. "Was it like that?" she whispered, her eyes searching Callie's.

Callie couldn't answer. Her voice was trapped in her throat. The kiss was too much to wish for and so unexpected that for a brief moment she thought that maybe she'd imagined it. If Katie only knew how long she'd wanted to be with her—to hold her, to feel her flesh next to hers and to kiss her lips. She looked into Katie's eyes, now seeing the unmasked fear of what she'd just exposed about herself.

Katie ran a shaky hand through her hair. "I'm sorry, maybe I shouldn't have done that." She moved away. "Please don't think...maybe I should go home."

Callie watched the color drain from Katie's face and realized that Katie misread her silence as dislike. "No...no," she quickly whispered in a raspy voice. "It's okay." She placed a trembling hand on top of Katie's, staring into her sea-green eyes and losing herself in the wonder of everything that made Katie what she was. Now those eyes held the promise of something special. "What do you want from me, Katie?" she whispered.

Katie tenderly put her free arm around Callie's neck and drew her closer.

Callie felt Katie's fingertips tremble as their lips met. This

time neither one of them pulled away as Katie's tongue softly
pushed Callie's lips apart until their tongues met. A raw, primitive
hunger Callie didn't understand engulfed her, and she couldn't
suppress her desire even if she wanted to. Her yearnings for
Katie gushed through every fiber of her being, almost suffocating
her. Katie pressed her body closer as Callie wrapped her arms
around her. She wanted to stay locked in Katie's embrace for the
rest of her life.

A soft moan escaped from Katie's throat. Finally, Katie
released her; their eyes met, searching, seeking, and knowing
that what they needed they could only get from one another.

"I...I wanted to do this for so long...you don't know." Katie's
voice shook. "I was so scared."

Callie brushed her fingertips over Katie's cheek. "Katie, me,
too, but I was afraid to tell you how I felt. I wanted to tell you, but
I didn't know how. The first time I saw you in school...I know it
sounds stupid...but it's the truth, I felt something . . . a
connection...it was like something zapped me and I couldn't get
you out of my mind or stop thinking about you."

"I know," she nodded. "I felt it, too." She put both arms
around Callie, then lovingly kissed her forehead, her chin, her
eyes, her neck, and finally her waiting lips as her hands gently
massaged her back. The yearnings Jill had aroused in her were
nothing compared to what Katie was bringing to the surface.

"Oh God, Katie," she moaned. "This feels so right." She
ached for her so much that she thought she'd die from want, but
what that want was she didn't know; only that she needed to hold
onto this moment forever.

"Yes," Katie whispered close to her ear, "It is right."

Slowly they undressed one another, then Katie held her at
arms length as she stared at her naked body. Callie's eyes traveled
over Katie's body, marveling in her beauty. She'd seen Katie's
nakedness before in sneaked peeks, but had never dared touch
or look too long. Finally, Katie held her arms out. Callie willingly
went into them, pressing her body close to Katie's, her throbbing

bare breasts touching Katie's as Katie lightly ran her fingers over Callie's skin, teasing and taunting her until she thought she would explode. Her mind wavered between fantasy and reality as Katie gently lay her down on her bed. Slowly and timidly, they touched and explored every inch of one another. Callie's senses wavered between rapture and terror at the same time, but she couldn't stop even if she wanted to.

Later Katie cradled her in her arms as she rested her head against Katie's shoulder. Katie lightly stroked her hair. All the emotions and turmoil Callie had kept buried inside tore through her and warm tears began to fall, softly at first, then harder. She couldn't stop them as they freely flowed from her eyes as her shoulders gently heaved.

"What's wrong? Did I hurt you?" Katie asked softly, brushing the tears from Callie's cheeks. "I would never hurt you."

"No," Callie sobbed. "It was beautiful and more wonderful than I ever dreamed it would be." She took a ragged breath. "I'm just so happy. You make me feel so loved, wanted and cared about, Katie."

"You are," she whispered, caressing her cheek. "Forever. We'll be together forever."

Chapter 8

Katie and Callie's friendship flourished and deepened with each passing day. Their lovemaking enhanced and cemented their bond, and they found themselves wanting to be together twenty-four hours a day, but that wouldn't be possible until they turned eighteen and could be out on their own. That still left them a little over three years, and they were a couple in every sense of the word as far as they were concerned. Their only anguish was not being able to emerge like an accepted couple in public, but only in private, making the time they had together precious and sacred to them, drawing them even closer as they planned their futures together.

School was hell for both of them, and Callie's heart still skipped a beat each morning when Katie appeared at her locker. When they'd pass in the hall it was all Callie could do to refrain from grabbing onto Katie and pulling her close just to feel her soft warm skin next to her own. Now more than ever, they had to be on guard.

Michelle and Debbie were finally beginning to accept the fact that Katie was going to remain a part of Callie's life, but if they ever found out how close they really were it would be the end for both of them. Callie continued to date to throw any suspicious minds off their trail. She broke up with Jack a few weeks after she and Katie first slept together, and was now seeing a boy from the next county named Nick. Katie didn't want her to date, but Callie reminded her how skeptical it would look for her not to be going out with the opposite sex and instead spending almost every weekend with her. Katie finally agreed that they'd have to play society's game for now, and they made certain that they appeared to the world like any typical fourteen-year-old best friends—riding bikes, racing, walking, going to movies or listening to music. No one could ever be privy to their secret. They lived in their own private little world where they would retreat and draw strength and acceptance from one another as they shut out the harshness and cruelty of the real world. Callie still hung out with her friends and Katie would sometimes join her or stay home secure in Callie's love for her. Callie knew that Katie was a true loner and preferred to remain that way, and it didn't matter to her, just so Katie was happy. But she still tried to convince her over and over that she needed to date because it seemed odd to many people that a girl with her looks showed no interest in boys. Katie wasn't worried, rationalizing that people probably assumed she enjoyed her solitude too much, but Callie worried just the same.

They lived for the nights they could be together. When the lights went out and Callie cuddled up next to her, she found tranquility and security in her arms, and all her pain and suffering melted away. On an emotional level they felt much more mature than their years would allude to. They had their ups and downs and were always careful to respect one another's feelings. They never argued loudly, but calmly discussed what was on their minds and made a pact never to go to sleep angry with one another. Neither of them could bear to see the other in any type of pain, emotional or physical.

Callie thought by now Katie would have invited her to her home, but she hadn't, and the time came when Callie had to let her know how she felt. She watched Katie as she lay sprawled on the carpeted bedroom floor, a pillow propped under her elbow, her eyes glued to 'Gunsmoke'. Callie loved watching her. The awkward stages with their bodies growing and changing didn't seem to affect Katie, and she was rapidly developing into a feminine beauty, with every new curve falling into the proper place. Her long, beautiful eyelashes, and of course those green eyes Callie loved, were an annoyance to Katie. She hated her femininity and was only totally relaxed and at ease when in her jeans and flannel shirt.

Katie gently pushed a fallen strand of hair from her cheek.

"Katie, we need to talk," Callie said softly.

"Can it wait till after the show?" she asked, keeping her eyes on the screen.

"Sure."

"How about the next commercial?" She turned her head slightly and flashed Callie a big smile.

"It can wait till after your show," she answered with a playful wink. She grabbed her notebook and lay on her stomach on the bed. Seconds later she heard Katie turn off the TV. "It can wait till later, Katie. It's okay."

"No, it's not." Katie lay down beside her and propped her face in her hands. "What's up?"

Callie looked into her gentle eyes. That was one of the traits that endeared Katie so much to her heart. She'd give up her own pleasures if she thought Callie needed something. Callie felt guilty and leaned over to give her a gentle kiss. "Watch your show and we'll talk after."

She shook her head. "It wasn't very good tonight."

Callie knew she wasn't being truthful, but she didn't let her know that she was aware of it. "Katie, do you have any problems with me?"

Her eyebrows rose. "Of course not. Why would you think that? I love you—you know that."

Callie searched her eyes as she pulled herself to a sitting position. "Then why haven't you invited me to your house? Katie, is something wrong with me? I can only come to the conclusion that there's some reason you don't want your mother to meet me. Are you ashamed of me or something? Is that it?"

Katie quickly sat up. "God, Cal, no. Please don't ever think that." She scooped her into her arms. "I've wanted to ask you over so many times, but whenever I come here and see everything you have I feel so ashamed."

"Ashamed of what, Katie?" She pulled away from her embrace and stared at her.

Katie swallowed hard. "Because my mom and I are so poor. You're used to nice things. I live in The Projects, I don't have much of anything, and you're used to having everything. It makes me feel like I'm the one who's not good enough for you."

Callie's eyes widened. "That's real good, Katie. So now you think I'm materialistic. How many times have I told you that I don't care what a person has or where he lives but it's what's inside that's important? Especially you, Katie. You could live in a fucking tent for all I care—just so you're still with me."

"You've said that a lot of times." She lowered her eyes.

"And you think I was lying?"

"No," she whispered. "I really want you to meet my Mom."

She put her hands on Katie's shoulders. "Katie, I want to know everything about you. I want to know what your bedroom looks like, the bed you sleep in when you're not here. I don't give a shit how much stuff you have or don't have. I only want you."

"I'm sorry."

"Katie, you have nothing to apologize for. Someday when we're on our own we may not have a lot right away, but at least we'll have each other, so who gives a fuck about all this material shit? If I had to choose right now, I would give up everything for you. And you'd better damn well believe it, too."

"I know you would." She gave Callie a penetrating look. "What about you?"

Callie raised her eyebrows. "What about me?"

"You're not being one hundred percent truthful with me either."

She frowned. "What have I done?"

She cleared her throat. "Let me refresh your memory. Ever

since we became friends, at least twice a month you go off on these secret trips, but you never say where you're going or who you're going to see. If I ask questions then you deliberately change the subject. How do you think that makes me feel? Especially since we started making love. How do I know that you don't have another girlfriend somewhere?"

Callie shook her head in disbelief as tears stung her eyes. "I don't want anyone but you, Katie. The only person I go out with is Nick and it's not like I really want to. You know that."

"But you have fun with him."

"Yeah, I do, but as a friend...that's all." She sighed. "Why don't you finish watching 'Gunsmoke'? I've got a book report to finish."

She wagged a finger at her. "See, that's what I mean. Every time I bring up something you don't want to talk about, you conveniently avoid it or don't want to talk anymore."

Callie's eyes misted. "Katie, I'm going to tell you, but not right now. Please trust me on this. Do you think I enjoy keeping anything from you?"

"Sometimes I don't know how you really feel. You're romantic and everything, but you never say the words."

"What words?"

"The words 'I love you'. I'm always saying it to you, but you never once said it back to me."

"Yes, I have. I always tell you that I feel the same about you."

"That's what I mean. You always say you feel the same or 'me too', but never the phrase. Don't you think for once I'd like to hear those words, too?" she asked in a pained voice.

Tears swam in Callie's eyes. She did love her; her heart and soul overflowed with love for her. Katie deserved an explanation, and she had to convince her of her undying love and devotion. The only way she could do that was to tell the truth. Katie deserved to hear it no matter the consequences to Callie. "Katie, I'm afraid to say those words."

She looked surprised. "Why? If you love me, you should be able to tell me. It's easy. I would like to hear you say it just once."

She took a shaky breath. "Katie, the only love I have ever known has been painful until I met you."

"What are you talking about?"

"My family. Families are supposed to care about each other, but I get kicked around all the time. My mother has never said she loves me. I know my Dad loved me even though I don't exactly know how I know that, but I always seemed to feel his love. I loved my Dad even though I was a little kid when he died and couldn't really have known him, but I felt so connected to him. My mother said it was my fault he died."

Her eyes softened. "How could it be your fault since you were just a little kid?"

"She said I was bad. According to her, I was bad from the minute I was born, and because I was bad, my Dad died. That has always stayed in my memory. I know it sounds dumb, but stuff stays with you sometimes, especially when someone says something that hurts. It just doesn't leave your mind. Know what I mean?"

She nodded.

"It's like every time I love something, it dies or disappears. Look at my cat."

Blackie had died in the early fall. Callie found his lifeless body by the bushes in the backyard near her bike early one morning. She was devastated, but Katie had come right over and took care of him while Callie cried her eyes out up in her room. Later Katie came up to get her and they went to his burial spot, and Callie said her good-byes to him. Katie was always there for her in her time of need.

Katie's eyes clouded. "It's not because you loved them that they died, Cal. Whoever killed your cat was sick!"

"I couldn't stand it, Katie, if something happened to you or I didn't have you with me."

Katie stroked her hair. "I'm not going anywhere. We're spending our lives on earth and whatever comes after together, remember? Together forever." Her voice was soft. "Please, just once let me hear those words?"

Callie gazed into her eyes. An unknown fear clutched her chest as she spoke. "Katie, I do love you so much. I wish you could see inside my heart all the love there just for you."

Tears came to Katie's eyes and she pulled her close. "I love you, too, Cal," she whispered.

"I want to tell you where I've been going. I don't want to hide anything from you any more." Her voice cracked.

"It hurts bad, doesn't it?" she quietly asked.

She nodded as a shudder tore through her. "You have to promise me something first."

"What?"

"You can never tell anyone ever what I'm going to tell you," she insisted.

"Are you in some kind of trouble?" she worriedly asked.

She rubbed her temples. "I...I don't know what to do. Promise me this is only between us. I need your word, Katie."

"I promise." She grabbed her hands. "No matter what it is I'll help you. We'll get through it together."

Callie squeezed her hands.

Katie bent toward her then kissed her cheek. "Don't tell me now, Cal. Only tell me when you're ready. I'm sorry I put pressure on you."

Callie threw her arms around her neck. "Please just don't think I'd ever cheat on you. I'll never want anyone else."

"I know," she whispered in her ear. "And I won't bring this up again."

"I will tell you soon, Katie," she promised.

"Okay."

Chapter 9

Callie was surprised a couple of weeks later when Katie announced with a bright smile that it was high time she met her mother. It was a long time in coming, but she knew that it meant that Katie was now ready to share every part of herself with her.

"I want you to spend the night," she announced. "I mean if you want to."

Callie gave her a big smile. She'd been waiting so long, and now the excitement was overpowering, making it difficult to concentrate on her classes. She was nervous, hoping Katie's mother would like her and if she did that would make their eventual announcement of their feelings for one another easier.

They already knew it would be difficult when the day came to reveal their true feelings for one another to their families. Callie knew what her family's reaction would be, but she sensed that Katie's mother would be more open-minded. At least that was what she perceived from Katie's interpretation of her mother, but she also knew that people sometimes said one thing and meant another. It was blatant hypocrisy, even though they would usually deny it. Callie intended to spend the rest of her life with Katie, and it would be easier if one of their parents gave them some emotional support. Knowing the closeness between Katie and her mother, she didn't want to do anything to sever their tight bond. She wondered how it must feel to be so close to one's mother like that, but she didn't envy her as much as she was happy for her. In any event, Callie hoped Mrs. Johnson liked her.

At the end of the day, Callie stood by her locker, waiting for Katie. She smiled as they left the school.

"How come you never mentioned in the beginning that you knew I lived in The Projects?" Katie asked as they entered the sidewalk to her apartment complex.

She shrugged. "Where you lived never mattered to me. You should have come right out and told me, but since you didn't, I just figured that after you got to know me you'd see that it was you I cared about and not where you lived."

She let her breath out in a rush. "I was afraid if you knew where I lived when we first met, you wouldn't want to hang out with me. Then after we started going together, I still felt like my place was such a dump compared to yours, even though you told me it didn't matter to you."

"And now I hope you know that it's you I care about, and not what you have or don't have."

"I've known it for a long time." She flashed a bright smile. "Especially after that talk we had."

"Just don't ever forget it, Katie."

Withered leaves crunched under their feet as they walked, and the darkening sky and brisk snap in the wind threatened snow. "My Mom knows about us, Cal." Her head was slightly bent forward as she walked into the stiff wind.

Callie laughed. "Well, I certainly hope she knows that we're best friends or she'd be wondering why we spend so much time together."

"That's not what I mean." Her voice grew serious.

"Well, what do you mean, then?"

Katie deliberately kept her face turned away from Callie's. "She knows that we're more than best friends."

Callie stiffened. "You mean that she knows about…"

She nodded. "I was gonna tell you, but I didn't know how."

Callie stopped dead in her tracks and Katie stopped, too.

She met Katie's eyes, seeing the frightened look at her reaction. "God, Katie. I thought that was sacred between us."

"It is, Cal. Don't be mad at me, please."

"Katie, how could you tell your mother that we're fucking? I know you and her are close, but for God's sake, why did you have to tell her?" Her voice rose a little higher than she intended it to.

"It's not like I just came out and told her. We were talking...I guess I talk about you so much that she just figured it out."

"Now I'm scared to meet her."

"Don't be. She's cool with it."

"Oh come on, Katie! It had to be a shock to her," Callie said.

She shook her head. "No, it wasn't. I think she suspected it."

Callie raised her eyebrows. "Why would she suspect that? Were you with someone else before me?" She tried to keep the jealousy out of her voice.

Katie's eyes widened. "No, I swear. I was never with anyone before you. You were my first and I was your first. You know that."

"Well, did you have a crush or something on a girl?"

"Probably no more than you did," she said slyly.

Callie wasn't in the mood for joking. "I can't back out now." Her voice was tight. "Or believe me, I would," she said firmly.

"But you're mad at me, right?" Katie anxiously asked.

"Let's just say I'm not real thrilled with you at the moment." She gave her a hard look. Katie knew her well enough to know that she was incapable of being angry with her for any length of time.

"I'm sorry. Just please don't be upset with me. I hate it when things aren't right between us."

Callie longed to feel Katie's warm hand covering hers, or Katie's arm around her shoulder, and she knew Katie wanted to comfort her as much as she wanted to be comforted by her. But since they didn't have the same options as opposite sex couples, gazing into her eyes and seeing all the love there just for her had to be enough. And right now, it was enough. "Me, too," Callie answered with a weak smile. "I love you too much to stay mad at you."

Katie grinned.

"Hi, Mom, we're here," Katie called as they stepped inside the apartment. Callie followed her into the living room and looked around. The living room and dining room were actually one large room, and she guessed the kitchen was off the dining area when she heard the distinct clanging of pots and pans coming from that direction. She saw a staircase to the left of the living room. It was a small·apartment, but comfortable and homey. Callie noticed a few baby pictures adorning one wall.

"That's me," Katie said with a smile.

"You were so cute, what happened?" Callie teased.

Before Katie could respond, Callie heard a voice behind her.

"You must be Callie. I'm happy to finally meet you," Mrs. Johnson said.

Callie turned and beheld the most beautiful woman she'd ever laid eyes on. Callie's own mother and none of her friends' mothers looked like this woman. She looked young enough to be Katie's older sister, not her mother. "It's nice to meet you, Mrs. Johnson." She shook the hand the woman extended.

"Oh no, please call me Bobbi," she beamed. "My Katie has told me so much about you that I feel like I know you already. Please sit down and make yourself at home. Can I get you anything?"

"No, thank you." Callie stiffly sat on one end of the sofa and Katie sat on the opposite end. Bobbi seated herself in an easy chair. Her warm smile quickly put Callie at ease. Bobbi had long, flowing blonde hair and the bluest eyes Callie had ever seen. She was small boned and petite, with deep-set eyes and beautiful, high cheekbones. Looking at her made it obvious where Katie got her looks.

"Katie tells me that you come from a large family."

She nodded. "Yeah, counting my mother there's eleven of us, so it can be pretty noisy at times. I spend a lot of time in my bedroom, especially when Katie comes over." She realized what she'd just said and blushed. She glanced at Katie who smiled back at her. "I meant . . . uh..." she stuttered, making her face flush even more. " Katie's not used to all the racket."

"I know what you mean, Callie," Bobbi quickly said, studying her closely. "I know that you and Katie share more than just a friendship."

Callie's cheeks blazed as she helplessly looked at Katie, noticing that her face was almost as red as Callie knew her own must be.

"Mom," Katie cried. "You're embarrassing us."

"I don't mean to," she apologized, leaning back in her chair. "You two realize that you need to be very careful, don't you?" Her voice wasn't patronizing, but filled with motherly concern. "Much of the world looks differently on same-sex couples. A lot of people may not be kind, and might say and do things to hurt you."

"I know," Callie whispered. "No one knows or suspects."

She kept her eyes level with Callie's. "Does your mother know?"

She shook her head. "We talked about it a couple of years ago and..." She lowered her eyes. "She doesn't understand who I really am."

"I'm not condemning your and Katie's love, Callie. And I'm sorry that your mother doesn't understand you, but it's difficult when your child is different."

"How did you feel when you found out that Katie liked girls?"

She laughed. "I put my arms around her and told her that I would always love her, and that what ever felt right to her must be right."

"I wish my mother would at least try to understand."

"You can talk to me any time you need to, Callie." She looked at Katie. "I've already explained to Katie how cruel people can be. I just don't want to see you two get hurt." She focused on Callie again.

"You aren't upset that we..." she couldn't finish the sentence. " I...I never felt right until I met Katie."

"No, I'm not upset. I just want you two to be happy and safe. As far as I'm concerned, you're no different than any other couple in love. Love is love." She smiled warmly. "Katie's not much of a socialize or talker, but I knew something was up when she talked incessantly about you and started spending every second she could with you. It was quite a drastic change." She glanced at Katie. "You're a good influence on her, Callie. I've never seen her so happy."

Callie grinned.

"Oh, Mom," Katie said self-consciously.

"Now, honey, I'm sorry for making you blush, but you obviously do have good taste."

Katie slid closer to Callie. "Thank you for understanding us, Mom."

"It means a lot to us," Callie added gratefully.

"Well you have to remember that you two are very young, and emotionally you've taken on a big load. Once sex enters the picture, no matter if you're straight or gay, it can change things."

"We love each other, Mom. We want to be together forever." Katie squeezed Callie's hand.

"I'll always be here for the both of you," Bobbi said.

Chapter 10

The weeks passed swiftly, and Callie began spending almost as much time at Katie's house as Katie did hers. Bobbi treated her like a daughter, and Callie found herself confiding in her and pouring out all of her pent-up emotions—emotions that had been locked inside for so long. She felt free, and for the first time in her life like she truly had a purpose and mattered to someone. Bobbi gave her the mothering that she'd longed for all her life.

Christmas was fast approaching, and it would be her first Christmas with Katie. Callie was like a little kid waiting for Santa Claus. Christmas and Easter always made her happy anyway, because those two holidays always found her mother and family in joyous moods and they treated her pretty good then—almost like they cared about her—so she took advantage of their good humor for as long as it lasted.

When the first big snow came Callie and Katie ran around like little children, making snow angels, and having a snowball fight. Callie showed Katie how to layer her clothes for warmth and instructed her on the proper boots to wear. Callie loved the snow for the first couple of days; then the novelty began to wear off as the temperatures began to dip and a cold northerly wind took hold dropping the daytime temperatures to single digits and below. She constantly worried about Katie, especially when she insisted on walking home late at night in the frigid temperatures, and would anxiously wait by the phone for Katie's call telling her she'd arrived safely.

Callie loved their nights together as they'd shiver and cuddle closer together under the blankets and quilts for warmth. The wind and snow swirled outside, whistling through the eves and pushing against the house with such force that they swore the house was going to blow down. Sometimes they'd stand by the window and watch as the moonlight glistened on the falling snowflakes, making them look like sparkling diamonds falling from the sky. It was a magical wonderland.

Every day Callie's love was growing stronger and more intense, and she couldn't imagine life without Katie. They had to continuously be on guard, so Callie spent time with her friends, occasionally inviting Michelle to spend the night. Katie wasn't keen on it but accepted it because they had no other choice. Callie's mother made frequent comments about the fact that Callie seemed to be avoiding her friends for Katie. She made it a point to spend even more time with her friends, either at her house or going to the movies and the diner, even though she ached to be with Katie. When they were apart she felt like a piece of herself was missing, and only Katie made her feel whole again.

In school Callie still met her friends in the girls' room for their usual morning smoke and chitchat. Katie always came along with her. Her friends talked to her, but not in the same way they did with one another, but still Callie was thankful that at least they were treating her better, not making her the butt of their jokes anymore. Katie was dressing better and talking a little more, which took some pressure off Callie, who thought Katie fit right in with the crowd. She was happy, and this was going to be the best Christmas she'd ever had.

On Christmas Eve Callie gave Katie a bracelet, wishing to have something special engraved on it but instead opting for just her name. Someday she would get her one with what she really wanted to say from her heart, but for now this was all she dared to do. Katie gave her a wood carving of her astrological sign, and it meant more to Callie, knowing that Katie had made it with her own hands.

She longed to spend the night with Katie, awakening Christmas morning in her arms, but satisfied herself with the reality that in a few years they'd be able to.

"I remember a poem I wrote because I was so tormented with my feelings for you, and about what it would be like to make love with you," Callie said. "I went crazy every time I saw you and memorized every word you said, the way you looked, and your smile."

"Read me the poem."

Callie blushed. "It's not very good."

"Please read it to me," Katie said softly. "I want to know how you felt."

Callie grabbed her notebook and nervously cleared her throat. "Okay, here goes. ' You live deep my heart, my love concealed because of fear/I see you and I long to touch, knowing that our love can never be/Still longing, hoping, wanting you, your touch is all I yearn for/My heart grows heavy as my tears begin to fall, in the deep of night where no one can see/The wounds all come out to play, taunting me with your image on my mind/I slumber as the sun begins to rise; only then can we be together.'"

When she was finished, she raised her head and looked sheepishly into Katie's eyes.

Katie grabbed her hands. "I felt the same way about you," she whispered. "I was so scared to say anything to you, but I couldn't stop thinking about you either. But you've put all those feelings down on paper."

"Did you like it?"

She nodded. "I loved it." She kissed her cheek. "The frustration of wanting to touch you and tell you that I was so in love with you was almost too much to bear at times."

Callie ran her fingers through Katie's hair. "I know. It was torture, wondering if you felt the same way. It was too much to hope for and when it did happen, and after our first time together I wrote another poem."

"Read it to me, Callie. I want to know exactly how you felt."

She smiled. "I wrote it later that night. You were sound asleep, and I remember waking up and thinking it was a dream until I saw that both of us were naked." She blushed. "Well, anyway, this is how I felt. 'Your heart touched mine but you didn't see/My tortured soul trying to reach out to grasp your love/Fear froze the embers of my being/Lost in time I couldn't see/Two hearts entwined for all eternity/I was too frightened to take a chance on fate/But you were patient and waited for the right moment in time.'

"That's how I felt, Katie. If you wouldn't have made the first move, I don't know what would have happened."

"I do."

She looked wide-eyed at her. "What?"

"You would've let me know eventually."

"I don't think I could have. I was too afraid of losing your friendship if you didn't feel the same way."

She grinned. "Maybe I was already picking up your signals."

"Was I that obvious?"

"Not at first, but you talk in your sleep sometimes."

Her face reddened. "I do? What did I say?"

"You called out my name, but it was the way you said it."

"Why didn't you tell me?"

She laughed. "What could I say? You were sleeping. I still had to be certain."

"Is that why you asked me if I'd ever kissed a girl?"

She nodded. "I knew if I got you to open up, I would know one way or the other."

"What if I wouldn't have told you?"

"I would've found another way to find out."

Callie grinned. "I guess we could wonder forever, but all that really matters is that we found each other."

"Yes, and we'll never be apart. Always together on earth, and in eternity."

Chapter 11

The wind was howling when Callie quietly stole into her bedroom. The lonesome whistling echoed throughout the house. She parted her curtains and gazed out at the parking lot below, seeing the headlights of his car casting an eerie glow on the snow-covered pavement. He glanced up towards her bedroom window, then slowly backed out of the parking space and headed off into the night. She felt sick to her stomach, having just been violated in every sense of the word. "Damn you God!" she screamed inwardly. She wanted to shout and shriek at the injustice that was repeatedly inflicted on her body every time he came near her. She'd kept this secret locked inside for six long years. Tonight was the worst, though. She'd finally found the courage to fight back and had paid the price. Blood trickled down her leg. She hugged herself, feeling like her insides had been ripped out.

Hot tears poured from her eyes as she thought of the irony of her situation. How could Katie's touches be so tender and sweet and his so harsh, demanding from her body what it was incapable of giving? He had no right to insist from her what he always did. He'd started molesting her when she was eight years old. She'd tried to fight him off and threatened to tell someone what he was doing to her, but he warned her that if she did, people she cared about would end up dead. He'd stolen her childhood, left her hurt, and confused. As the years wore on the abuse became more frequent, until the day came when he'd fully penetrated her. She was sick for days afterward, wanting to rid her body of his vile filth.

She longed to tell someone and have an end put to this ravage of her body, but there was no one she could trust. She worried that no one would believe her anyway and would think she'd gone along with it willingly, since she'd been letting it go on for so long. What they wouldn't see was that she'd been just an innocent child who was the victim of a heinous crime. What kind of sick, demented man would be attracted to a child who could be the age of his own daughter if he had one?

Shame and guilt ate away at her, and she'd been on the verge of ending her life when Katie came like a ray of sunshine, giving her hope for a new future. Katie was the lifeline she needed to hang on to, and when she found out that Katie was also gay, she knew her life could now be complete. The loneliness and isolation dissipated when she and Katie were together. She was no longer alone in this harsh world.

She'd spent years wondering why she'd even been born if she was only to be despised, taunted, sexually violated and different from her friends, but having Katie's love for the rest of her life made all of it bearable. She needed to tell Katie what was going on with all of the mysterious trips, but she didn't know how to explain it. Katie hadn't brought up the subject again, but Callie still saw the questions in her eyes. She longed to get this burden off her chest.

How she wished to be in Katie's arms at this very moment. She needed to be held and comforted by her, but she couldn't let Katie see her in her present condition. She walked into the bathroom and filled the tub with the hottest water she could stand, then stepped into the tub, sucking in her breath as the water touched her wounds and sent a quick shot of excruciating pain through her. She gently dabbed at her body with the washcloth, being careful of the parts he'd bruised. She looked down at her swollen vaginal area.

She sucked her breath in again as she toweled herself dry

and put on fresh clothes. She was walking back into her bedroom when the phone rang. She rushed to the family room and quickly grabbed it; Katie's voice greeted her on the other end of the line. Just hearing her voice eased some of Callie's pain.

"Hi, Katie, I just got out of the tub. What did you do all day?" she asked, trying to keep her voice controlled.

"Nothing much. What time did you get home?"

"About an hour ago."

"Did you miss me?"

"You'll never know how much." She blinked back hot tears welling up behind her eyelids.

"Are you okay, Cal?"

She swallowed the lump in her throat. "I'm fine."

Katie hesitated. "No you're not," she sighed. "I can tell by your voice that something's wrong."

"Everything's fine, really. I can't wait to see you tomorrow, Katie. I do miss you."

"Callie, tell me what's wrong. Please?"

"Katie, there's nothing wrong. I'm tired and I'm going to try to get some sleep. I'll see you tomorrow. I love you."

"Callie, wait. I'm coming over."

She chewed her bottom lip. "No, Katie, you can't." She couldn't let Katie see her this way. If Katie came over she'd have to tell her, but right now she was mentally and emotionally exhausted and didn't think she could do it.

"Don't you want to see me?" she asked in a low voice.

"God, yes, but not tonight." She shut her eyes, squeezing back the tears that threatened to fall.

"I'm worried about you."

"I'm okay," she said in a wobbly voice.

"Please let me help you, Callie. Something's wrong. I need to see you. We made a vow to be there for each other always. Please don't shut me out anymore," she pleaded.

"Katie, I'm so afraid," she sniffed.

"My Mom's home tonight. I'll have her give me a ride over."

Before Callie could answer, the line went dead.

Callie paced back and forth across her floor, every few minutes peering out of the window. Twenty minutes later, she saw Bobbi's car stop and watched as Katie hurried out of the car to the house. Minutes later she stood in Callie's bedroom with her arms tightly wrapped around her.

"My God, what happened to you?" She looked at Callie's red, tear-swollen eyes. "Tell me what's wrong."

Callie trembled, holding tightly to her, almost afraid to let go. "Promise me that you'll never leave me."

"Never." Katie softly brushed her cheek with the back of her hand. "Who did this to you? Who hurt you?" Her eyes searched Callie's. "Please tell me who did this to you."

Callie shuddered.

"Does this have something to do with those secret trips you go on?"

She nodded.

"Please tell me who is doing this to you. It's time to share that pain with me, Cal."

"I'm so afraid, Katie."

Katie took her hands and led her to the bed, where they sat side-by-side. "Don't be afraid. Please, just tell me what's going on."

"I don't want to lose you."

Katie put an arm around her shoulder. "You'll never lose me. There's nothing that will ever make me go away from you." A tear fell from her eye. "Now tell me who the hell did this to you?"

Callie buried her face in Katie's chest and cried like she'd never cried before. All of the pent-up pain and humiliation exploded within her and poured out through her tears. Katie rocked her as she cradled her in her arms, patted her back and stroked her hair.

When Callie's sobbing had finally subsided, she blew her nose, then got up and walked to the window. She kept her back to Katie. "It started when I was eight years old."

"What started?" Katie softly asked.

"Sexual stuff." She heard Katie's sudden intake of air. "I was so afraid. All I remember is how much it hurt."

"Oh my God!" Katie cried.

Callie sniffed. "I've had everything imaginable shoved in me. I...I couldn't stop him," she said in a broken voice.

Katie walked over to her and held her. "Please, tell me everything." She kissed her hair. "I want to help you."

Two hours later Callie had finished giving Katie all of the abhorrent details. They both cried and held one another as Callie relieved the past six years, grateful that Katie was there for her. She was relieved to finally share this terrible part of her life with someone.

Katie paced back and forth across the floor with a beer in one hand and a cigarette in the other. She abruptly stopped in front of Callie. "I'd like to kill him," she said through gritted teeth. "That bastard has no right to do this to you!"

Her anger frightened Callie. She'd never seen this side of her before, but she knew how she'd feel in Katie's place. "Could you hold me, Katie?"

She was at Callie's side in a flash, setting the beer on the floor and crushing the cigarette in the ashtray. She enclosed Callie in her arms. Callie heard the wild thumping of Katie's heart, then suddenly Katie began to cry softly at first then harder. Callie pressed her body closer.

"I'm so happy you're here with me. I feel so safe with you."

Katie bit her bottom lip. "I'm gonna get that bastard one way or the other. He's never gonna put a hand on you again," she promised.

"There's nothing we can do."

"Would your mother listen if you told her?"

She smirked. "Yeah, right. She thinks he's the greatest thing going. He's almost like a part of the family." She let her breath out. "I guarantee that she would find a way to twist everything around and make it my fault."

"Well, we'll think of something." She wiped her eyes. "But I'll be damned if I'm going to sit back and let this happen to you again."

"I feel so dirty."

"No, don't. It's not your fault," she soothed.

"Remember that you promised to never tell anyone."

"I know."

Callie stretched, then yawned. "I'm so tired. You're spending the night aren't you?"

She patted Callie's hand. "Of course I am. I already told my mother I'd probably stay over."

"I...I can't..." she sniffed. " He hurt me there and I'm bleeding."

Katie winced. "Shh, I know. I'll hold you while you sleep."

Katie settled back against the pillow then Callie laid her head on Katie's chest knowing she would finally be able to rest in the only place that gave her peace.

***

Katie held Callie closely, listening to her soft breathing as her thoughts and emotions pillaged her mind. She fought back her tears and, finding it fruitless, finally let them freely flow from her eyes. When Callie stirred in her sleep Katie held her even tighter. She never wanted to let her go, feeling the need to protect her from all the pain in the world. There had to be a way to make that pervert stop abusing her; she didn't know how, she only knew that she would somehow find a line of attack.

The thoughts of what he'd done to Callie made her want to vomit. She tried to push the images from her mind as bile from the pit of her stomach slowly inched its way up her throat. He had no right to touch her. He took the body she loved and defiled it.

It was obvious from Callie's bruises that she'd tried to fight back. He wouldn't get away with this, and she would never let him get near Callie again. She gagged as the images continued to penetrate her thoughts. She took a few deep breaths until the wave of nausea left her.

She held Callie tighter. She was falling deeper in love with Callie as each day passed. She had never imagined in her wildest dreams that Callie's secret would be anything like this. She'd been violated in every sense of the word, and Katie felt violated, too.

She could almost feel Callie's pain and knew it stemmed from their deep body, mind and soul connection. No, she would never again allow anyone to hurt Callie. She inhaled deeply, then planted a soft kiss on Callie's forehead. "I'll figure something out," she promised.

Chapter 12

"I'm not hungry, Mom," Katie said, pushing her plate aside. "I'm going to give Callie a call."

"Katie, wait a minute. Can we talk for a few minutes?" Bobbi asked. "I'm worried about you, honey."

Katie smiled faintly. "I'm fine. You don't need to worry about me."

Bobbi set her fork down. "Something's wrong. You barely eat, and I know you're not sleeping well. Honey, I hear you in the night crying," she said in a worried tone.

"I really am fine, Mom."

She sighed. "Are you and Callie having problems?"

"No, we're so happy."

"Then what is it, Katie? You've always been able to talk to me. I want to help you. Something's wrong. Are you sick?"

She shook her head, then got up and walked over to her mother's chair. She knelt down and put her head in her mother's lap. "I wish I could tell you, Mom, but I promised Callie I'd never tell. I gave her my word."

Bobbi frowned. "Is Callie in some kind of trouble?"

"No, Mom."

"Then what is it, honey?"

"I can't tell you. I wish I could, Mom, but I really can't."

"Let's go sit on the couch and have a talk."

Katie stood up and followed her mother, then sat next to her, looking down at her hands and nervously twisting them together.

"What's going on with Callie?" she softly asked. "You know how fond I am of her."

"I know, but I promised her I'd never tell anyone what she told me."

Bobbi's brow puckered. "Sometimes, Katie, we need to share with someone. Now, whatever Callie told you is obviously too much for you to handle. I'm sure Callie will understand if you confide in me."

She quickly shook her head. "No, Mom, she'll never forgive me if I do."

Bobbi touched her shoulder. "Honey, you can't keep on this way. It's making you sick."

She blinked hard and gulped as she began to cry.

Bobbi put her arms around her. "Honey, what's wrong?"

She sniffed. "I can't tell," she cried. "But it hurts so bad."

"Has something happened to Callie?"

She nodded slowly. "I'm just so angry," she gulped.

"Please tell me. Maybe I can help," Bobbi softly prodded. "Callie wouldn't want to see you suffering like this."

"I know," she sniffed again. "Promise that you won't tell anyone else ever."

"I promise, honey."

She shuddered. "Callie's being..." She swallowed the lump in her throat. "Someone is doing things...I can't," she choked. "It's awful, Mom!"

Bobbi inhaled deeply. "Katie, is Callie being sexually abused?"

She winced.

"Oh dear God!" she exclaimed. "The night you asked me to drive you over to Callie's, was that when you found out? You haven't been yourself since."

"Yes," she whispered. "He beats her up, too. I don't know how to help her. I'm scared to be away from her because I don't know when he'll show up."

"How long has this been going on?"

Katie covered her mouth with her hands as Bobbi held her. "Mom, I think I'm going to be sick."

"Come on, honey, I'll help you."

***

Later Katie lay in her bed. She couldn't sleep, and the aspirin she'd taken for her throbbing headache hadn't kicked in. She hoped her mother would keep her word and never let on to Callie that she knew about her abuse. Katie had never broken her word to Callie before and she never intended to. Trust was something that Callie held sacred, and she understood why Callie had kept that terrible part of her life hidden from her. Katie still couldn't shake her feeling of helplessness. Her only consolation was that maybe her mother would come up with a solution and Callie would never have to suffer again.

***

Bobbi fixed herself a cup of tea and flicked on the channel 4 news. She listened to the usual tragedies, but her mind stayed focused on Callie's personal affliction. She had to find a way to help her. She would have to confront Callie about what Katie had told her at the risk of jeopardizing the beautiful mother-daughter relationship she and Katie shared, but there was no other way. Katie couldn't carry this burden alone, and surely Callie would understand that. The three of them would try to find a solution and finally put an end to this nightmare.

Bobbi felt sick when she realized the horrendous pain, suffering, and humiliation Callie must have endured at the hands of that monster for all these years. She shuddered, thinking what if it had been Katie being viciously abused. She would feel the same way she did now. Callie was like a daughter to her and she couldn't tolerate this aberration. It would only end up completely destroying Callie.

***

Katie shivered as she reached the apartment. "I'm glad you're spending the night, Cal."

She grinned. "I know how we can get warm."

Katie gave her a sly wink, then said with a laugh. "I think we need to go to bed early tonight."

She laughed. "Sounds good to me."

Bobbi greeted them at the door. "Hello, girls, and how was school today?"

They both made a face, then looked at each other and broke out in laughter.

Katie hung their coats in the closet. "Aren't you working tonight, Mom?"

"No. I have to work a double shift tomorrow so I'll be gone before you two even get up."

"Okay, what's for supper?" She shut the closet door.

"I made a big pot of stew and some homemade bread."

She tossed her hair. "Good. I'm starved."

"When aren't you hungry?" Callie teased.

Bobbi smiled. "So, what do you two have planned for tonight? Anything special going on?"

Katie shrugged. "Nothing really. It's freezing out, but we'll find something to do."

Callie knew that the cold affected Katie, and she never minded what they did as long as they were together. Besides, she loved spending time at the apartment because Bobbi made them feel relaxed and comfortable, and it wasn't a big deal if they sat close together or held hands. They could be themselves. There were very few places they could do that without worrying about someone seeing them.

Callie looked at Katie. "It's too cold to go anywhere tonight and only going to get colder. Why don't we just stay in, watch TV, and make some popcorn?" She saw relief flood Katie's eyes. "Besides, Bobbi, I can show you my new dance steps," she said, flashing Bobbi a mischievous grin. "Maybe we can even get Katie to loosen up and dance with us."

"It sounds like fun," Bobbie replied distractedly.

Callie noticed that Bobbi wasn't her usual bubbly self and wondered if she was coming down with something.

"You don't mind staying in, Cal?"

She squeezed Katie's hand. "I don't mind."

They walked into the living room. Callie and Katie sat next to one another on the sofa, and Bobbi in her easy chair. "I heard we might get a blizzard this weekend."

Callie nodded. "By the looks of the sky we're going to get something." She watched as Bobbi nervously folded and unfolded her hands. "Is something wrong, Bobbi?" she finally asked.

She quickly shook her head. "No, everything's fine. I just have a lot on my mind today. And storms make me so uneasy."

"Just be careful driving to work tomorrow, Mom," Katie said, flicking on the TV to a game show and immediately becoming absorbed in it.

"I will."

Callie glanced at the screen, then stole a look at Bobbi. Something was definitely bugging her, and Callie figured she'd tell them eventually. They sat in silence for the next fifteen minutes, Katie being the only one focused on the TV program. Every so often Katie would laugh at something on the screen and break the uncomfortable silence. Bobbi's quiet mood didn't seem to affect her, or maybe she hadn't noticed her mother's anxiety, Callie thought.

After the program ended, Katie flicked the channels searching for another program. Bobbi shifted in her chair. "Katie, could you please turn off the TV?" she suddenly asked. "I'd like to talk to you girls."

"Sure, Mom. What's up?" Katie asked brightly, flicking the set off.

She twisted her hands. "Callie, I'd like to ask you something," she began slowly.

Callie became alarmed at the serious tone of her voice. She wondered if she'd done something to offend her.

Katie jumped to her feet. "No, Mom, not now," she pleaded.

Callie looked at Katie, who had obviously picked up on a signal, but Callie was still in the dark. Katie paled like she'd just seen a ghost. "What's the matter, Katie?" She turned to Bobbi. "Have I done something wrong?"

"Oh, no, honey," Bobbi quickly assured her. "I just want to talk to you, that's all."

"Mom, no, please," Katie begged. "You promised."

Callie pulled Katie's hand. "Sit back down. What's the matter with you, Katie? Your Mom can ask me anything. She knows that."

"Callie, please don't be upset with Katie."

She raised her eyebrows. "I'm not upset with Katie." She squeezed Katie's hand. "She hasn't done anything."

"She's told me some things…"

"Mom, no!" She quickly grabbed both of Callie's hands. "Callie, I know I promised you—"

"What things?" Callie asked suspiciously, seeing the fear in Katie's eyes. She wondered what Katie was so afraid of.

"Callie, you need to talk to someone about what's been going on," Bobbi said in a pained voice.

"Everything's fine," she assured her. "I'm getting good grades and taking some advanced classes."

"Let's go upstairs and listen to some music until supper," Katie suggested, pulling Callie towards the staircase. "You can practice your new steps before you show Mom later. I'll practice with you," she said in a rush.

Callie raised her eyebrows. "You hate the way I dance."

"I don't hate it, I just can't move like you do."

"You've never wanted to practice with me before. Why are you in such a hurry to now?" she asked with a laugh. "We can practice after, Katie." She turned her attention back to Bobbi. "If I've done something wrong, please tell me. I can't change it if

I don't know what it is and you know, Bobbi, that I would never do anything to hurt you."

"Oh, no, honey, you've done nothing wrong. I just want to remind you that I'm always here if you need to talk . . . about anything."

"I know. I think of you like my Mom most of the time. And since I plan to be around forever, I guess it's like you really would be my Mom." She grinned, then noticed the sadness in Bobbi's eyes.

"Thank you."

"What's the matter, Bobbi?"

"Callie, sometimes it's difficult to share unpleasant situations. But you need to remember that it's not your fault. You did nothing wrong." She winced. "It breaks my heart to think of you being sexually abused for all these years."

Callie's jaw dropped at her sudden proclamation. Katie grabbed her hands, but she quickly pulled herself free, seeing the withering look Katie gave her mother. "You told, Katie? You promised," she whimpered. "I trusted you." Her bottom lip trembled. "Not you, Katie." She brushed the tears from her eyes. "You were the only person in this whole stinking world I could trust."

"Callie, you've got to believe me. I didn't want to tell. Honest." Tears sprang to her eyes. "I only wanted to help you," she moaned.

Callie shook her head back and forth. "No," she sniffed. "Maybe everything you've been telling me is just a pack of lies." She bit her bottom lip to control the trembling. "Who else did you tell?"

Katie sniffed. "No one," she mumbled.

"Tell me!" Callie demanded. "I have a right to know!"

"No one, I swear!"

"Callie, you have it all wrong. Katie couldn't handle knowing what you were going through. You don't know the hell she was suffering. I didn't know what was wrong with her, only that something was, and I forced her to tell me. Believe me, she didn't want to and tried not to, but I forced her." She let her breath out in a rush. "Callie, she cried like a baby when she told me. It crushes her to think of how you've been so violated. It's killing me, too. You've got to listen to me. Please calm down and listen to reason. She told me because she loves you, dammit! How do you think I feel? You're like a daughter to me."

"But she broke her promise to me. A person's word has to stand for something." She looked at Katie. "You should have at least asked me if it was alright to tell your mother."

Katie put her hands on Callie's shoulders. "I didn't know what to do," she cried. "How do you think it was making me feel? I couldn't protect you," she moaned.

Callie pushed her away then ran to the closet, retrieved her coat and quickly put it on. "I'm going home. Don't call me, Katie. I never want to talk to you again."

"No, Callie, don't say that. I love you!" Katie cried. "Please listen."

"You're not going anywhere, young lady," Bobbi firmly said. "We need to discuss this. You have to talk about this, Callie."

Callie looked into her eyes. "I...I can't talk about this right now," she whispered in a broken voice.

"You need to, honey. Now take off your coat and sit down. We'll figure out what to do," Bobbi said softly.

She shook her head. "I can't. I can't trust anybody anymore."

"Callie, please don't go," Katie pleaded. "I'm sorry. I'll do anything to make it up to you. Please!" she pleaded. "Anything you say."

"No. I need to be by myself. I need to think," Callie sobbed, heartbroken at Katie's betrayal. She longed to be in her arms right now, but Katie had let her down like everyone else always had. She was empty; there was nothing left inside and she couldn't stand the pain. She sobbed harder, her breath coming in short gasps.

"It's freezing outside, Callie. Please stay like you planned to do. Katie and I only want to help you. Quit being so damned stubborn and let us help you. If we didn't care about you, we wouldn't be trying so hard to help you now."

She took a ragged breath. "What I've been going through is degrading, and I never wanted anyone to know. I can't believe you'd break your promise to me, Katie. I thought we had something special together, but it's just a game to you. We have nothing together now. It's over." She felt a crushing pain as her heart broke. "How could you do this to me, Katie?" she sobbed, opening the door. "I'm sorry, Bobbi, but I have to get out of here."

Katie grabbed her arm, trying to get her back inside. "Please, Callie, talk to me," she cried. "I...I can't stand to have you mad at me. Callie, I love you! "

She looked into Katie's eyes. Tears were streaming down her face. "I can't ever trust you again."

"Yes. Yes, you can. I'm sorry, Cal. Tell me what I can do to make things right between us."

"I never want to see you again."

Katie backed away. "No, Callie, please don't say that. You don't really mean that."

She swiped at her nose, seeing the frozen expression on Katie's face. "I mean it, Katie, we're through."

Katie covered her mouth with her hands, then ran up the stairs, her sobs echoing throughout the apartment.

Bobbi grabbed Callie's shoulders. "I'm not letting you go anywhere in this condition, dammit! I care too much about you." She wrapped her arms around Callie. "I'm going to help you. Honey, what happened to you shouldn't happen to anyone and it's not your fault. You've got to believe that."

***

Katie threw herself on her bed as tears poured from her eyes. In her heart she knew that Callie didn't mean a word she said, but still her words wounded. She loved Callie so much it hurt. She knew Callie felt her love. They were so connected that most times they knew what the other was going to say before the words were even spoken. She didn't think she'd be able to stand it if Callie ended their relationship. What would she do if she did? She'd never be able to survive that excruciating pain. She wished her mother hadn't said anything, but even though she had, she couldn't be angry with her. She was only trying to help. Deep down Katie had felt relieved to share her heavy burden with her mother, and she felt sorry that Callie didn't have the same warm relationship with her own mother. Katie's mother anguished over Callie, and at least she recognized that what they shared was more than just a crush or puppy love. She respected their feelings for one another.

Katie looked at the empty spot next to her, thinking about the nights Callie had lain here wrapped in her arms and where she was supposed to be tonight. "No, Callie," she cried. "Don't leave me."

Chapter 13

Bobbie held Callie close, cradling her like a baby in her arms and gently rocking her back and forth as Callie cried until she had no tears left to shed. She patted, then tenderly rubbed Callie's back. Katie had told her about Callie's back problems and mentioned some other things that no child should have had to endure, but the worst was the sexual abuse. Bobbi was livid thinking how for six long years Callie had endured this unspeakable pain, but even worse had no one to turn to.

She acknowledged early on that Callie had been a stranger to any kind of normal love, and the only real love she'd ever known was the love and affection Katie bestowed upon her. Bobbi had come to see the gentle sensitive side of Callie, even though she'd never approved of the heavy drinking. She encouraged Katie to kindly point out to Callie that she consumed too much alcohol, especially for her tender age. Bobbi feared Callie would develop a severe problem either with the alcohol or with her health some day. She knew Callie wasn't into any hardcore drugs, but she suspected that the girls smoked pot and made it perfectly clear that it wasn't allowed in her home, and if she found any they would face severe consequences.

The more Callie frequented her home, the less drinking she seemed to do, and she observed Callie slipping into what was a typical teenage routine, sipping one of Katie's homemade milkshakes which Katie seemed to be making more often. It greatly relieved Bobbi to see a drastic reduction in the amount of alcohol Callie usually consumed.

Bobbi thought back to Katie's birth, a lump rising in her throat with the memory of the first time Katie had been placed in her arms. She looked at Katie's innocent, beautiful cherub face as her heart swelled with a love that only grew stronger with each passing day as their mother-daughter bond grew and strengthened. She'd never understand how a woman who had just given birth couldn't bond with the fragile, defenseless human being she had just given life to. Her bond with Katie had begun the moment she'd found out she was pregnant.

When Katie's father deserted them, Bobbi devoted herself to making the best life she possibly could for Katie. The move to New York had been rough on Katie, but she thought more opportunities awaited both of them after her job in Virginia was eliminated after twelve years. She wanted Katie to get the best education possible, and she'd heard that the educational system was one of the highest rated in the northeast. She hadn't let on to Katie that the move terrified her almost as much as it did Katie. She was leaving behind everything she'd known, but she'd never be more than a common factory worker in their small hometown in Virginia.

The move to New York, though, was not what she'd expected. She missed the warm hospitality of the south and found the friendliness of the northeast to be almost virtually nonexistent, at least as far as she and her daughter were concerned. She figured she'd have to do much adjusting and soon realized that those she met weren't necessarily rude, but in such a hurry that everyday common courtesies usually were something no one took much time for, with too many other things all ready occupying their limited time.

She hadn't been surprised when Katie came to her one day shortly before their move, confused over her attraction to girls. She'd suspected it for quite some time with the questions Katie asked through the years. They sat and discussed Katie's feelings, and Katie eventually confessed that she didn't like boys for anything more than friendship, but that girls made her feel strange inside, like she wanted more than just friendship from them. Bobbi gently explained to her how she needed to keep her sexual preference to herself until she met someone who felt the way she did. She explained that many people may not be open minded enough to understand her preference and may say or do unpleasant things to her if it were public knowledge.

"Is it wrong, Mom? Is something wrong with me?" Katie had asked. "I don't know why I feel this way." Bobbi had given her a hug, assuring her that if that was how she felt, then it was normal for her to be attracted to girls, just like it was normal for Bobbi to be attracted to men. There was nothing wrong with having the feelings that she did; it was just the way she was made and it was all right to be different.

She was already painfully aware that Katie's homosexuality isolated her from others as she tried to fit in with girls her age. She knew that Katie suffered alone, but Katie would find someone to share those feelings with. When Katie came home from school her first day in New York talking about Callie and in the following weeks continued talking incessantly about her, she knew that Katie had her first crush. She cautioned her about not moving too fast, especially when Katie confided to her that she didn't know if Callie felt the same way about her which only further confused Katie. She saw the longing in Katie's eyes and knew that her fragile heart could easily be broken. Katie anguished because Callie had a boyfriend, but she confided to Bobbi that Callie didn't appear to be very interested in him.

Bobbi suffered along with her daughter through her first yearning love pangs, happily recalling the day Katie gleefully announced to her that Callie felt the same way about her that she felt about Callie. The bright twinkling, dancing light in her eyes was like a spark ignited by something Katie had never known. She was on the threshold, ready to embark on a journey as she and Callie explored their sexuality together. Bobbi was elated that Katie had found her first love and guided her as much as she was able to.

***

Callie stirred, bringing Bobbi back to the present. "Do you feel better, honey?"

She cleared her throat and dried her eyes. "I'm sorry, Bobbi. I'm just so scared and upset."

She stroked her shoulder. "You don't need to apologize to me, honey. I can't even begin to imagine what you've been through. We'll figure out something. Katie and I are going to help you through this, and whenever you're upset or something happens to you, I want you to come to me."

She looked at Bobbi through blurry eyes. "I didn't mean to hurt Katie. I love her so much, Bobbi, you know I do, but she'll never believe me now." Fresh tears welled in her eyes. "Why does everything have to get so screwed up?"

Bobbi saw the love in her red, swollen eyes. "I know you love her, Callie, but sometimes words cause more pain than any physical blows ever can. I'm sure that Katie knows you love her, too. You realize that she was only trying to help you, don't you?" Her eyes searched Callie's. "She'd never hurt you in a million years."

"I know," she said in a low voice.

"You have to tell her how you feel. She's upstairs crying her heart out, and if I know my Katie, she's probably convinced herself that you'll never see her again."

"I can't stand being without her, Bobbi."

"Go to her, honey," she softly said.

Callie looked over her shoulder and flashed Bobbi a smile as she climbed the stairs. She quietly opened Katie's bedroom door and saw Katie curled up in a fetal position on her bed. Her shoulders moved up and down. Callie bit her bottom lip as she crept over to her and gently touched her shoulder. "Katie, I'm so sorry for saying those horrible things to you." She brushed the hair from Katie's cheek, feeling the wetness of her tears, then softly grazed her lips across Katie's cheek as she climbed onto the bed, pressing her body close to Katie's as she wrapped her arms around her. "I love you so much it hurts, Katie," she whispered in her ear. "I'm so sorry that I hurt you. I need you." Fresh tears spilled from her eyes.

Katie turned over and buried her face in Callie's neck. "Don't ever leave me," she sobbed.

Callie felt like her heart would burst wide open with the love she felt for her. She was ashamed for taking her pent-up frustration out on Katie. The anger that had been a part of her for so many years had been directed at the wrong person, and it was only because she wasn't familiar with someone's help having never been offered any before. But more importantly, she'd never been the object of anyone's unconditional love before. Katie loved her no matter what, and truly did want to be by her side in the good as well as the bad times.

"I could never leave you. Please tell me that you forgive me. I can't stand to see you hurting, especially knowing that I'm the one who hurt you. I need you and I always will."

Katie sniffled. "I love you so much," she said in a muffled voice. "I've been so scared for you. My mom's the only person I told. I swear. I would never deliberately hurt you. I didn't want to break my promise."

Callie raised Katie's face until they were staring into each other's eyes. "I know you didn't tell to hurt me. I was too stupid to see what it was doing to you. I don't know what I would have done if the situation had been reversed. I couldn't have stood it for as long as you did."

"I wish it was me instead of you."

"No, Katie! Don't ever say that. I would never want done to you what was done to me."

"Then you know how I feel. I can't stand it and it's got to stop."

"Your Mom is going to try to help us figure something out, but right now I just want to be close to you." She nuzzled her neck. "Please hold me, Katie."

She put her arms around her. "I was so scared," Katie shivered.

"Of what?"

"That you were going to break up with me."

Callie kissed her brow. "Leaving you would be worse than death. I don't think I could survive the pain of losing you. I would be dead inside."

"You still staying over?"

She smiled through teary eyes. "You can't get rid of me that easy. I've been looking forward to tonight all day."

She took a deep breath. "Let's not ever fight again. I can't stand it."

"Me either. I love you so much, Katie, sometimes I think more than you'll ever know."

***

Bobbi set the table and waited for the girls to come downstairs. Now that Callie's horrible secret was out in the open, she needed to come up with a plan that would protect Callie from any further abuse. Going to Callie's mother was out of the question, but there had to be someone who would listen and help. For the first time, Bobbi understood why Callie drank so much. She doubted the child enjoyed alcohol that much, but it had been the only thing available to numb her mental grief.

She wondered how much more damage it had really done to Callie, emotionally and physically. As Callie endured the normal woes of puberty with her ever-changing body, it must have been worse knowing that night after night she would be subjected to those unwanted attacks. She shuddered. Everyday the television news and newspapers were filled with similar tragedies, and she wondered what made someone so sick that he could do that to a child. All Bobbi knew for sure was that if Katie had been the pervert's victim, she would have castrated the bastard herself without batting an eye.

The apartment had grown quiet, leading her to assume that the girls had patched up their differences. If not, she was sure she would have heard some high-pitched squealing and crying. This was the first time she'd ever known them to have a disagreement, and she hoped they'd never have to face anything like this again. Their deep love for one another would strengthen them. She would never quite understand the type of love they shared, but she totally accepted it. Love was difficult enough to find, and they seemed to have found the love that was right for them with each other.

Chapter 14

Callie lay on the bed, listening to Katie singing a silly song she'd made up, her long fingers strumming the guitar. She laughed. "You're gonna be famous for sure." She slid off the bed and walked over to the window, peering out at the parking lot below.

"What do you want to hear next? I'm taking requests, so if you don't tell me now I get to make the next choice again," Katie said with a laugh in her voice. "How about a love ballad?" She strummed a few chords, softly humming, and when Callie didn't answer she set the guitar down and walked to Callie's side. "What's the matter, Cal?" Her eyes traveled to the car in the parking lot. She put her arms around Callie. "Is that his car?" she angrily asked. "He's here?"

She numbly nodded, then looked at Katie with fear in her eyes. "It's him. It's the day he usually comes around." She swallowed hard. "I…I can't—"

Katie's jaw twitched. "You're not going with him. I'll see to that."

"I'm scared, Katie."

She squeezed her shoulder. "You're staying at my house tonight. Come on, let's go."

Callie quickly threw some things into a bag, then followed Katie downstairs. As Callie was exiting the back door behind Katie, a strong, callused hand clamped down on her arm.

"Where're you going?" he asked. "I thought we'd go for a ride. You've been avoiding me."

"I'm staying over night at my friend's house," she said evenly. "I've got to go." She pulled her arm free.

He sneered, his eyes mocking her. "Who are you all dolled up for?"

She looked disgustedly at his small beady eyes and receding hairline. His potbelly grossly hung over his belt, with his tee shirt only reaching to his navel. "I've got to go."

"Not so fast...I have a special night planned for you."

She saw the lust in his eyes. "I don't think so."

Katie had been listening outside the screen door, but now stepped back inside. "Come on, Cal, let's go." Her voice was firm as her fiery eyes swiftly met his.

"And who are you?" he asked, looking her up and down. "Have we met? Where've you been hiding her, Callie?"

Callie knew that look in his demented eyes and it made her want to throw up, remembering how many times he'd looked at her that way before thrusting his unwanted cock in her. Thinking of him ever doing to Katie what he'd done to her made her stomach lurch. "It's none of your business who she is," she spat out.

He laughed, and when he did the stubble on his unshaven face moved up and down on his chubby chin. He laid a heavy hand on Katie's shoulder. "Are you a new friend of Callie's?"

Katie promptly shook his hand off. "You'll never touch Callie again, do you hear me?" she hissed through gritted teeth. "Leave her the hell alone. You're old enough to be her father. Why don't you find someone your own age?"

A look of amusement appeared on his round face as his beady eyes kept a steady gaze with Katie's. "No, you've got it wrong. See, you don't know Callie like I do. This sweet young thing is nothing but a cheap whore. She begged me for it. She can never get enough."

Callie watched as Katie's eyes turned into two smoldering dark slits. At any minute, Katie would lose self-control. That's what he wanted. "Let's go, Katie," she said. "He's not worth it."

"Katie's your name, huh? That's a pretty name." He moved

his rough hand up her arm. "How would you like to go for a ride since Callie here doesn't want to go?"

"In your dreams, asshole," Katie repulsively replied.

His eyes flashed. "Sometimes dreams come true."

"I know what you've been doing to Callie, and you're never going to touch her again. If you do, you'll be sorry."

He laughed. "It takes two, you know. She loved it, ask her." He nodded towards Callie.

"If you touch her again I'll tell everyone that you tried to get me in your car. I'll tell them that you tried to rape me, and don't think that I won't do it."

He glared at Callie. "Get the hell out of here. You're not worth it...just a couple of sluts."

They slammed the door and walked to Katie's apartment, both wrapped up in their own thoughts, but when they arrived, they filled Bobbi in on what had just taken place.

"Do you think he'll try anything again, Callie?" she worriedly asked. "He doesn't sound too balanced."

She squinted. "I hope not. Maybe now that he knows other people are aware, he might be afraid to try anything again. At least I hope he doesn't."

"Just be careful. Both of you," Bobbi warned. "Katie, maybe you shouldn't have said anything to him."

She adamantly shook her head back and forth. "No, I had to let him know." She looked at Callie. "I think he's scared, don't you, Callie?"

"Yeah, but I still didn't like the way he was looking at you and trying to get you to go with him."

Bobbi bit her bottom lip. Her brow creased. "He needs to be locked up."

"I know," Callie agreed. "I wonder if he's done this to other girls, and if he'll find a new one to start abusing."

"I just care that he won't be coming after you anymore," Katie stated.

Bobbi was thoughtful. "Callie, I know it wouldn't be easy,

but can't you go to the police and tell them? They have to help you."

Her eyes grew wide with fear. "No, I don't ever want anyone to know what he did to me." Her eyes pleaded with Bobbi's. "I couldn't take it. People around here are sick and would twist it all around."

She squeezed her shoulder. "Honey, I'm not asking you to do anything except to be careful and on guard. If he starts in on another girl then hopefully she will be able to turn to someone for help."

She gave Bobbi a hug. "Just knowing I have you and Katie in my life makes me feel safe."

***

In the weeks that followed, Callie finally settled into a somewhat normal routine and was comforted that he didn't come around much anymore. When he did, it was when she usually wasn't home. That part of her life thankfully seemed to be over, but it would never be out of her mind. He'd left scars on her memory that would never fade; she was angry at what he'd stolen from her, and all of the lonely years of terror, torment, and humiliation he'd put her through. He'd made her feel so dirty, and she wondered if she'd ever feel completely clean again.

Katie made everything seem all right, and Callie cherished their time together, wishing she never had to be away from her. Time spent with Katie was what she lived for. She loved staying at Katie's apartment savoring the peacefulness and privacy it afforded them, but mostly the sense of family and belonging she felt when she, Katie, and Bobbi were all together. They were her family and fulfilled her with everything that had been previously lacking in her life. She belonged and was wanted.

She loved lying in Katie's big double bed on warm spring nights as a cool breeze from the river drifted in through the open window. She filled her lungs with the fresh river scent. Katie sacrificed a lot for her, and she always tried to get her to do the things Katie enjoyed so much. "You should go fishing tomorrow, Katie. It's going to be a nice day."

She shrugged. "What are you gonna do?"

"I'm not sure."

"I'd rather spend the day with you."

Callie yawned. "I've got to get a checkup. It's that time of year again."

"I'll go with you."

She gave her a quick hug. "Nah, you'd be bored sitting there while I get all these tests and x-rays. He'll probably just give me the newest painkiller on the market for my back. I'll call you when I get home, though, and we can do something. Maybe we can see a movie. We haven't done that in awhile. I'll even let you pick out the movie," she said with a smile.

"Okay, that'll be a switch. I'll have to see if there's a western playing." She returned her smile.

Callie rolled her eyes. "Okay, I promised you could pick it out."

Katie squeezed her hand. "I was just thinking."

"Uh-oh, what about?"

"Do you like cooking?"

"Yeah," she smiled. "Just don't ask me to sew. Why? Is there something you want me to make?"

"I just wanted to know who was going to do the cooking when we get our apartment."

Callie laughed. "Always thinking about food."

"So. I love to eat, I just hate cooking."

"I know, and I already planned to do the cooking or we'd starve to death!"

"Hey, I'm not that bad. I can cook when I absolutely have to."

Callie looked carefully at her. "No, actually you're great at taking the leftovers out of the fridge and sticking them in the oven…but only if someone tells you what temperature and for how long."

Katie laughed. "Okay so I'm not much good in the kitchen, but I'm good at cleaning up and doing dishes when I have to."

Callie sat up. "Sometimes I look at you and wonder what kind of mother you'd make."

She grimaced. "No way would I ever want to be pregnant."

"I wouldn't mind if it was your baby."

She smiled. "Yeah, if that was the case I'm sure you'd be pregnant by now, and I could see you explaining that to everyone," she giggled.

Callie raised her eyebrows. "Oh come on, Katie, you don't think they'd understand if I said Katie Johnson got me pregnant?"

"Well, we'd sure as hell be famous and make medical history."

Callie sighed. "Well, it would be cool to raise a baby with you. We would be the coolest parents that baby ever had. He could be a writer, singer, guitar player and maybe we'd let him come up with some ideas of his own."

She laughed. "The way things are going, I'm sure some day they'll come up with a way to get pregnant without a man involved."

"Then I'll be the first one in line," Callie said enthusiastically.

***

Callie grabbed her jacket. "I'm done, right?"

"Callie, wait a minute. I want to talk to you about your tests," Dr. Jamison said, his fatherly eyes peering over his glasses.

"Sure." She frowned. "I've been feeling better, but my back still hurts some times."

"I know it does. I'll give you a prescription for the pain. I also want you to take some vitamins, and please try to eat more iron-enriched foods."

"Okay. Is that it?"

"There's something else we need to discuss."

"What?"

He removed his glasses. "Are you sexually active?"

Her face reddened. "No...why?"

"Callie, I'm asking you this privately. I promise that whatever you tell me will remain only between us. I won't tell your mother."

She shook her head in wonderment. "No, I swear, I'm not!"

He let his breath out in a rush. "You have some problems." He cleared his throat. "It's doubtful, Callie, that you'll ever be able to bear children or even become pregnant."

She scrunched up her face. "What's wrong with me?"

He patted her hand. "It's not life-threatening, but we'll periodically need to run more tests."

***

Callie sat across from Katie and sipped at a Coke. She popped some coins into the jukebox, then leaned back in the worn leather booth. She picked up her pack of cigarettes, took one out and lit it, slowly blowing the smoke out as the music started blaring.

"Cal, what's wrong? You've barely said two words all night, and when you're this quiet I know something's bothering you."

She smiled at Katie. "Nothing, I'm fine. Just a little tired."

Katie peered at her. "How were your tests? What'd the doctor say? Are you okay?" she asked worriedly. "You were supposed to get the results today weren't you?"

She shrugged. "Yeah, I'm okay." She looked around the almost empty room. In twenty minutes the place would be packed as soon as the show let out. "Want to get out of here? I don't feel like running into anyone."

"Sure. Want to go to my house or yours?"

"I don't care."

"What's the matter, Cal?" she whispered.

"Nothing."

Katie sighed heavily. "We promised no more secrets." She put her jacket on.

Callie slid out of the booth and followed her outside. They walked in silence through Main Street. Katie lit two cigarettes, then handed her one.

"We're going to my house. Come on."

Callie raised her eyebrows. "I think that's the first time I've ever heard you say what we're going to do without asking me a hundred times if its okay."

"Well, it's about time that I made some decisions."

She grinned. "Let's take the River Road. It's more private."

Katie grabbed her hand in the secluded darkness, entwining Callie's fingers with her own. "Will you tell me what the doctor said?" she asked in a quiet voice.

Callie held her hand tightly, then cleared her throat. "It's really no big deal."

"It must be if it bothers you."

She kicked a stone out of her way. "He said that I probably couldn't have kids, 'cause I'm messed up in my female organs."

"Will you be okay?"

"Yeah, it's not serious."

"But you wanted to have babies."

She shrugged.

"Maybe someday we could adopt a baby," Katie suggested.

"You always know the right thing to say to make me feel better." She held her hand even tighter.

"Don't ever forget it, Cal. I want us to share everything."

"We will," she promised. "Forever."

Chapter 15

Callie and Katie were ecstatic when they were assigned not only to the same school for work, but also to the same work team. Now they could spend some weeknights at one another's houses also. On the nights they weren't together, Katie showed up early the following morning to pick Callie up for work.

Callie bounded out of bed every morning, threw her clothes on, then went downstairs and had a cup of black coffee and a cigarette, tuning the radio to the pop station, but making sure the volume was turned down low. At exactly seven-fifteen Katie would appear, signaling her arrival with a light tap on the door. Callie was always near the door, anxiously awaiting Katie's arrival minutes before she was even due.

Sometimes Katie rode her bike; other times she walked the mile to Callie's house, and they'd walk the other mile and a half laughing, joking, and holding hands when the street was deserted. Sometimes they'd even boldly sneak a quick kiss. Callie always trembled at Katie's touch. She'd heard her friends discussing how the thrill and excitement at the beginning of a new relationship seemed to gradually lessen as time wore on, but Callie still felt the same tingle she'd felt when she and Katie had shared their first kiss. She assumed that it was different between boys and girls and was even happier for the excitement she and Katie shared.

At work they were split into groups and put into separate

classrooms. Callie and Katie were paired with a short, plump blonde named Karen who was a year behind them in high school. The other girl was a plain, tall, too-thin brunette named Barbara whom Callie had only seen in school but didn't really know.

Callie and Katie sat on one side of the worktable, Karen and Barbara on the other side. Karen had a loud, boisterous personality and talked almost incessantly. Occasionally Barbara would join in. Karen always had a joke to tell, and Callie laughed and told some of her own. Katie never said much, sometimes appearing uncomfortable with the chattering, and usually kept her head bent low, concentrating only on her work at hand.

One hot day they sat working, wiping the perspiration from their faces. "These little rug rats better appreciate these books," Callie laughed.

"Most of them will have the covers ripped off before the end of the first day," Karen grimaced. "After all, what can you expect from the porch monkeys' kids."

Callie laughed, then looked at the few book covers left in the stack. "I'm gonna get some more covers so we won't have to do it after lunch. Be right back."

**

Katie watched Callie leave the room. She hated being left alone in Karen and Barbara's company, especially Karen's. Karen made her feel self-conscious. She had nothing against them personally, but their constant silliness got on her nerves. She wished they could just work in silence once in awhile and cut out some of the senseless babbling. It seemed to her that Karen was one of those types of people who seemed to talk only to hear the sound of her own voice. Katie focused on her work. She'd be relieved when Callie returned.

"How long have you lived here, Katie?"

She looked up; surprised that Karen had even acknowledged her. "Over a year."

"I'd think you'd have lost that hicky accent by now."

"It's just the way I talk. I was raised in the south."

"Don't you have any friends?"

She shrugged. "A few."

"What about a boyfriend?"

"No." She wished Callie would hurry back so she wouldn't have to answer Karen's nosy questions.

"Don't you like boys?"

"They're okay."

Karen propped her elbows on the table. "Callie has a boyfriend."

"I know." She kept her eyes on the book cover she was putting on.

"Did you have a boyfriend at your other school?"

Katie sighed. "No"

"You look at Callie like you're in love with her."

Katie felt her face redden. "She's a good friend, that's all. She helped me get settled when I transferred here."

Barbara giggled. "You are so sick, Karen."

Karen laughed. "No really, watch Katie's eyes light up the minute Callie comes back in the room. She acts like such a dyke."

Katie felt like throwing up as she sat frozen to her chair, her eyelids burning. Her hand trembled as she turned the book over.

"What's the matter, Katie?" Karen prodded. "Are you upset because Callie has a boyfriend and isn't a dyke like you?"

"I'm back!" Callie announced, her arms laden with book covers. She set them on the end of the table, then took her seat next to Katie.

Katie kept her eyes low and nodded as Karen nudged Barbara, then proceeded with another of her insufferable jokes. She felt the hot stinging growing more intense behind her eyelids, but she couldn't cry—not in front of Karen.

***

At lunchtime they usually stayed at their workstations and ate their packed lunches amid more prattling. Callie always brought a thermos of hot black coffee and slowly poured a cup as Katie looked on in disapproval, pouring either milk or juice from her own thermos. Katie ate in silence, barely uttering a word. Callie was keenly aware that something was bothering her, but she couldn't ask her with Karen and Barbara sitting across from them.

Katie finished her lunch, then stood up and picked up their trash, depositing it in the wastebasket. "I'm going outside for a smoke," she said with a nod in Callie's direction.

"I'll have one, too." Callie followed her outside into the hot suffocating daylight.

"It's so humid," Callie said, mopping her face with her shirt as they stood at the side of the school under a tiny awning, which provided the only shade. "What do you want to do tonight, Katie? There's a new movie playing. I don't remember the name of it so I don't know how good it is." She lit two cigarettes and handed one to her.

She shrugged dejectedly. "I don't know. My Mom's got the night off for once and I was thinking of just staying home and spending some time with her. I haven't had a talk with her in a long time."

Callie smiled. "Yeah, that'll be fun. I love spending time with your Mom. She's so cool. You're so lucky to have her for your Mom, but then so am I," she said with a wink. "I'll have to show her my new dance moves. Maybe you can dance with me, too. You really are a good dancer, Katie. You've got a great style, and if you'd lighten up and relax I think you'd enjoy it more."

She threw her cigarette to the ground and squashed it out with her tennis shoe. "I think I just want to spend some time alone with my Mom tonight."

"I know. You already told me that. What time do you want me to come over? Hey, I know…I'll spend the night, okay?"

She shuffled her feet. "We'd better get back to work before we get bitched at."

Callie looked into her eyes seeing the pain and hurt there. "Katie, wait. Did I do something wrong?" she asked, surprised.

She shook her head. "No, everything's fine. It's not you."

"Are you mad at me?"

She didn't answer, but quickly hurried back inside the school.

"Katie!" She ran to her side. "What did I do? Katie, I don't know what I did. Everything was fine this morning. What happened?"

She didn't answer as she rushed to the classroom and walked to her seat. Callie pulled her own chair out, then sat down. She picked up a stack of book covers and quickly began covering the books, finding it difficult to concentrate on even this routine, monotonous task. Something was wrong with Katie and she was determined to find out what it was.

Karen cracked a few jokes, but Callie only flashed her a pithy smile. She brushed her leg against Katie's, missing how Katie always did that to her. When she got no reaction she glanced at Katie, but Katie kept her eyes riveted on her work, ignoring her. She looked up and saw Karen peering at her with a strange look in her eyes.

"I love you, Callie," Karen said in a high-pitched mocking voice. Callie ignored her, but Barbara burst out in laughter. "Lighten up, Katie. God, there's nothing like being love sick."

Callie's eyes widened. "What the hell are you talking about, Karen?"

Karen and Barbara made kissing noises, smacking their lips against their arms.

"Knock it off, you're not even funny," Callie said.

"We're just kidding, Callie. But maybe you don't know the object of your friend's affections."

Katie quickly stood up, knocking her chair over. "I have to go to the bathroom." She ran from the room.

Karen snickered. "Callie, you'd better make sure your girlfriend is okay."

"Quite picking on Katie. She's okay."

She raced down the hall to the restroom and found Katie leaning against the radiator with a look of total desolation on her face. "What's the matter?" she whispered. "What did I do?"

Katie ran her hand through her hair. "Listen to what Karen and Barbara are saying. God, Cal, don't you know?"

Callie put her foot up on the radiator. "No, I don't. Ignore them. Everything was fine with you and me this morning."

"How do you think I feel?"

"I told you they aren't worth it. They're just trying to have some fun at your expense. If you let it bother you, they'll only pick on you more. Just laugh it off. We know the truth." She made a funny face. Usually Katie would laugh, but now she remained stone-faced. Callie took a deep breath. "Let's take the rest of the day off. I'm sick of this place."

"Okay. I'll be there in a minute."

She touched Katie's shoulder. "I'll be in the classroom. Don't ever let them think they got the best of you. If you do, then they'll keep on."

Callie walked into the room and gathered her things. "Where you going?" Karen asked.

"Home."

She nudged Barbara. "Where's your puppy?"

Callie looked questionably at her. "What?"

"Your puppy."

"I don't know what you're talking about, Karen."

Karen laughed. "Come on, Callie, she follows you around like a puppy dog."

Callie scowled. "She does not! Why don't you leave her alone? She hasn't done anything to you."

Katie walked over to the table and grabbed her things, then picked up Callie's thermos bottle. "You don't have to defend me, Callie. I can take care of myself."

Callie reached for the thermos. "I can carry it, Katie."

"What did you do, kiss and make up?" Karen asked

sarcastically, with a look of disgust on her face. "I love you, Callie," she mocked. "Let me carry your books for you."

Callie slammed out of the door with Katie at her heels. She stayed a few paces ahead of Katie, and noticed that Katie didn't try to catch up to her until they'd walked almost a quarter of a mile. Callie felt tears stinging her eyes.

"Cal," Katie panted hurrying to her side. "I'm sorry. Thank you for sticking up for me."

"It's okay," Callie answered, "but I would like to know why you acted so funny toward me."

"It's not you. It's me."

"I'm not following you."

She sighed. "Everybody likes you."

"No they don't. Come on, Katie, what's really wrong?"

Katie's eyes narrowed. "Karen called me a dyke."

"What? When?"

"When you went in the other room to get more book covers right before lunch. I can't stand her."

"Why didn't you tell me before?"

Her eyes shifted. "God, Callie, I thought you'd figure it out with what they were saying. I'm so scared of messing your life up...of messing our life up. Look how Karen was making fun of us."

"Ignore her. She's just trying to be cool. Do you want me to spend the night tonight?"

"Maybe we should quit spending so much time together until this blows over. I don't want to get you in trouble." Her eyes clouded. "What if your mother hears something? I don't want you to get sent away or us to be separated." Her eyes narrowed. "Callie, I wouldn't be able to handle it."

"Friends always spend time together. What if it was Michelle or Debbie I was with a lot of the time? Then no one would say a word. I used to spend loads of time with Dana, and then with Michelle, and no one thought anything about it. Besides, I have a boyfriend and everyone knows it."

"I just don't want anything to happen to us."

"It won't. We've been careful. So you still don't want me to spend the night?"

"I do, but I'm just scared."

"Don't be. We'll get through the next couple of years, then get the fuck out of this rotten town."

"I thought maybe you'd change your mind about us, especially with all the pressure from Karen."

"Katie, you don't know how happy I am that I met you. It was awful before I knew you. You know the feeling of being so alone and not fitting quite right anywhere. Whether we're together or not, we're still gonna want to be with girls. I think all this just makes us more bonded. It's not fair that we have to hide how we feel, but we do. When we go to New York City or somewhere else someday, we can be together with people who are just like us. We just have to keep remembering that living here right now isn't going to be forever. It's hard, but we've been through so much crap all ready. Now we're almost halfway there," she said with a grin. "Besides, Karen's a fat pig. No one will really believe her. I just wish things could be easier for us, and it really does frustrate me that we're not able to be like other couples."

Katie smiled. "We'll find a place to live and all of our friends will be just like us. It'll be beautiful," she said brightly.

Chapter 16

"Oh my God, guess what I just heard?" Michelle panted, rushing to Callie's locker.

"What?"

"They're gonna do a major locker search for drugs." Her eyes were as wide as saucers.

Callie shrugged. "They can't just raid our lockers."

"I'd get the booze out of there," she warned. "If they find anything illegal, you're busted."

Callie feigned surprise. "I don't know what you're talking about."

"Get off it. Everybody knows you keep a stash. We're not stupid."

"So you just look it," she teased, seeing the annoyance on Michelle's face. "I'm just kidding. So, when are they gonna do it?"

"Some time next week."

"Thanks for the warning."

Later Katie and Callie sat in Callie's room discussing the situation. Katie knew how much alcohol Callie kept in her locker and how much Callie needed it to make it through each day. They'd talked about it many times, and Katie had begged her to cut down on her drinking at least during school hours.

"Can they just rummage through our stuff like that?" Katie asked.

She nodded. "Yeah, we're just students, and they can do whatever they damn well please."

"That isn't fair."

"No, Katie, but it shows you how stupid they really are," she grinned. "They warned us."

"What are you gonna do?" she peered into her face. "Actually, maybe you shouldn't bring it anymore."

She looked in surprise at Katie's statement, then sighed. "I don't know what I'm gonna do. I can't keep it in my purse. I've got enough crap in there as it is." She frowned. "Hey, wait a minute, I've got an idea." She looked at Katie.

Katie looked at her evenly. "Oh no," she said shaking her head. "Every time you get an idea, Callie, I get dragged into something. Besides, you don't need to carry all that stuff in your purse."

"I need everything in there."

She laughed. "Of course you do."

"No, this is the perfect plan, Katie. You could carry a purse. We're in high school now, and it's about time you started carrying one."

She raised her eyes. "I hate purses. Besides, won't I look suspicious since I've been here over a year and I've never carried a purse?"

"No one'll even notice. Come on, just do it for me. We can meet after classes in the girls' room."

"Our classes aren't always near each other."

"Who gives a shit?"

She frowned.

"I'll wait for you in the bathroom. It doesn't have to be after every class. I'll check our schedules and see which classes are close."

She shook her head. "No, I can't."

Callie knew that she had to find a way to convince her. "Katie, come on. I'd do it for you."

"Right. I know what you'd tell me to do."

She gazed into her eyes, then gently touched her cheek. "Please? Won't you do it for me?"

She hesitated. "Okay, okay, but I still don't like it." She rolled her eyes.

Callie flung her arms around her neck. "Thanks. I have a lot of purses. We'll find the perfect one."

"I know how many you have, but they aren't my style."

She laughed. "How do you know what your style is when you never carry one?"

"Trust me, I know. I'll find something."

"Just make sure that it coordinates with what you're wearing," she advised.

"I will."

She hugged her again. "Thank you. You're the best."

"I hope we don't get busted," she said with a worried look in her eyes.

"Katie, I wouldn't ask you to do this if I thought we'd get caught."

"Somehow that doesn't make me feel better," she said apprehensively.

***

On Sunday Callie sat on Katie's bed, skimming through her forty-fives. "What purse are you bringing?" she asked.

"I didn't find one yet. I'll go through my Mom's. I told her I was going to carry one on Monday." She grimaced. "You know how she's always after me to act more like a lady. Well, she got all excited and wanted to take me shopping for new clothes and stuff." She scrunched up her face. "Look what you've done."

Callie smiled. "See, she knows what a good influence I am on you."

She squeezed her hand. "Why do I let you drag me into these things?"

"Because you love me."

Her eyes twinkled. "You're right."

***

On Monday morning Callie jumped off the bus and went straight to her locker. She waited for five minutes, but Katie was nowhere in sight. Katie had promised to meet her early at her locker. She wondered if Katie had chickened out. *No, she would never do that to me*, she thought. *She would have called. Maybe I told her to meet me in the girls' room first.* She was pondering her dilemma when Michelle and Debbie appeared hysterical with laughter.

"Oh this is too much," Michelle choked.

She was laughing so hard she looked like she would pass out at any minute. "What?" Callie raised her eyebrows. "Are you going to let me in on the joke?"

Michelle was doubled over. "You haven't seen her?" She glanced at Debbie.

"Who?"

She threw her hands up in the air. "You've got to see this. This is too much!"

Callie glanced down the hall, but still didn't catch sight of Katie anywhere. She was growing suspicious. "What are you two up to?"

"Nothing."

Debbie's face was red from laughing. "You're in for a big surprise."

"You two are absolutely nuts." Their laughter was contagious and she tried to keep from laughing herself especially since she didn't have a clue as to what was so funny. "I'm gonna go for a smoke."

"Okay," they giggled.

"Are you coming?"

"Yeah," Debbie answered. "We're coming."

Michelle chuckled all the way to the girls' room. "Just wait," she warned.

"You two are so strange," Callie said with a toss of her head as they walked to their usual stall. Callie leaned against the radiator, keeping an eye peeled for Katie, but there was still no sign of her. Everyone was either smoking or checking her makeup. Callie checked hers, then inhaled deeply from her cigarette. She was getting antsy. She needed a drink and time was running out. "So, did they start the locker checks yet?" she asked no one in particular.

"Uh-uh, they'll probably wait till we're in class," Michelle answered.

Terry walked over to them. "Nah, I heard that they did some already this morning."

"Junior or Senior High?"

"Random, they're just picking this one, then that."

Callie smirked. "What do they think they'll find? It's not like anyone's stupid enough to keep pot in their locker."

"What about the cigarette packs?" Terry asked.

"No one leaves their cigarettes in their locker. If they do, then they're pretty stupid."

"Yeah, but you keep pot in your cigarette packs."

"Not any more. It's too risky. The cops are always taking our cigarettes, probably 'cause they're too cheap to buy their own." Now she kept her pot stash safely hidden in her bedroom. Only she and Katie knew exactly where the hiding spot was.

Amid the chattering, Michelle started worrying about getting caught smoking.

Everybody laughed. "Big deal, like it's a felony. They'd have to expel half the school," Callie said. Everybody was still laughing when the warning bell sounded. Callie tossed her cigarette in the toilet, wondering whether she should be worried about Katie or angry with her. The room suddenly became deathly quiet. She slowly turned around, assuming a teacher had entered their domain, and shot a glance toward the entrance. Katie stood inside the door. The room immediately filled with snickering and laughter as Callie's jaw dropped. Michelle and Debbie pointed and laughed. Katie self-consciously caught Callie's eye, avoiding all the other eyes riveted on her as she stiffly made her way over to her.

Callie was at a loss for words. "Katie, what the hell is this?" she whispered.

Her face reddened. She looked like she was going to cry. Everyone stood staring and gawking at her. "This was all I could find," she said in a weak voice.

"Katie, it's a fucking suitcase...you could put your books in there." Katie was struggling with her pile of books under her other arm. Callie felt guilty for not comforting her, but how could she with everyone standing around staring at them? She couldn't stomach seeing Katie being the object of everyone's ridicule. "Just put it in your locker. It'll be okay."

"I tried. It won't fit...that's why I'm late." Her eyes widened. "I don't know what else to do."

Callie bit her lip to keep from laughing as she tried to put herself in Katie's place. She looked so alone and vulnerable, but it was the stunned expression on her face that made her look even more comical. She was dressed so cute and stylishly today, too, in a navy skirt and light blue sweater. Callie would tell her later how great she looked. She'd obviously gone to great lengths to look her best for Callie, always doing her bidding, and Katie needed her now to come to her defense, but like a coward, Callie froze. The 'purse' definitely did not complement her attire, being square shaped, made of some straw like consistency, and bright purple with large, god awful gaudy orange and green flowers. It was about three times the size of Callie's shoulder bag. She wondered how Katie even had the strength to carry it at all.

"Are you laughing at me too?" Her eyes flooded with tears. "Not you, Cal. I did this for you."

"I'm sorry," she whispered. Everyone was exiting the bathroom and racing to class. Callie opened the 'purse,' grabbed a bottle and took a long drink, then placed it back inside. "Katie, couldn't you find something smaller and less noticeable?" She tried to keep her voice even.

"This was the only thing big enough to hold all your bottles," she replied in a small voice. "My Mom mostly has evening bags and clutch purses."

Looking at her broke Callie's heart. She wanted so desperately to pull her into her arms and comfort her, but she couldn't here in the girls' room.

"I've gotta go," Katie finally said. "I'm already gonna be late and I have a test."

"Katie, thanks." Callie watched as she walked towards the door, the bag dragging her shoulder down. She pushed on the door with her free shoulder and slipped into the crowded hallway, back into the mocking faces and ridicule. Callie would make it up to her, but at the moment, she didn't know how.

After school when Katie didn't show up at her locker, Callie searched for her for fifteen minutes to no avail. It finally dawned on her that Katie had most likely escaped the building as quickly as possible. Callie would have done the same thing in her place. She hurried out of the building and stood in front of the school, scanning the busy street and finally spotting her across the street. Callie caught up to her. "Katie, slow down," she gasped. "Let me take your books."

"No thanks, I can carry them." Her shoulders were hunched forward.

"Come on, Katie. I'm sorry. Please don't be mad at me." She grabbed the books.

Katie stopped and faced her. "I'm not mad, just hurt. How could you do this to me?"

"I'm sorry." She lit a cigarette. "Want one?"

She shook her head.

"Can I come over?"

"Why are you asking? You never asked before. You always come over whenever you want to."

Callie shrugged. "I don't know. You don't seem like you want me around today."

"That's how I felt all day long." She blinked back tears. "Do whatever you want to do." She quickened her pace.

"Right now I need to get warm. It's ten below." She shivered. "Well, I guess I'd better start walking home. It's a long way in this weather." She waited for a response from Katie, but she didn't respond. "I guess you'd better take your books."

Katie glanced at her. "You're not walking home in this weather. Come on."

Callie smiled. "Katie, it wouldn't have been so bad if it wasn't the middle of winter. If it was June, no one would probably have even noticed." Actually with the monstrosity she carried they would have noticed no matter what season it was, but she hoped that made Katie feel better. "Why couldn't you have found something at least geared for winter?"

"I overslept."

"I thought you were going to find a purse last night."

"Well, I didn't. Let's just drop it, okay?"

"Sure. I'm spending the night, okay?"

"Why?"

"God, Katie, if you don't want me to, just say so."

"I don't care. It's your decision."

"Forget it. I'll only stay long enough to warm up." She looked at her. "I love you. Don't ever forget that."

"I want you to stay over."

Callie smiled. "Let's skip school tomorrow and spend the whole day together."

She grinned. "I'd like that."

Katie put her key into the lock, but before she could turn it, the door was quickly opened. "Mom, what are you doing home? I thought you had to work tonight."

"I'm working a split shift tonight, honey. I have to leave in about twenty minutes. Hi, Cal." She flashed a brilliant smile.

"Hi, Bobbi." Callie tried to move next to Katie to obscure the view of the purse so Bobbi wouldn't see it, but Bobbi's eyes had already lowered.

"What's that?" she asked with a cocked eyebrow.

Callie didn't know what to say.

"Kathleen, when you said you wanted to carry a purse, I hope that thing isn't what you took to school."

Katie looked at her mother but didn't answer.

"Let's put our coats in the closet," Callie suggested, hoping to divert the conversation away from the purse. "It's freezing out, Bobbi. You better bundle up."

"Thanks, honey, I will."

Katie picked up the purse and set it down in the living room.

"Sweetie, tell me you didn't bring this old thing to school. I have a closet full of pocketbooks. That decrepit old thing's been around since you were a baby. I used to pack your things in it when we went to the beach."

Callie saw Katie's left cheek twitch. "I...I . . . "

"Oh, Katie, I would have found you something." She looked at Callie. "Cal, you've got to take her shopping. You've got such good taste."

Callie nodded, thinking the worst was over.

Bobbi sighed. "Well, at least you only carried it to and from school. Thank God for lockers."

Katie shifted her weight from one foot to the other. "It wouldn't fit in my locker," she said through gritted teeth.

"Oh, no, honey, you mean to tell me—" She shook her head as the laughter she'd been holding back bubbled up from her throat.

Callie tried to control herself, but the minute Bobbi caught her eye she lost it and was practically rolling on the floor. Katie looked at her mother, then at Callie, before angrily turning on her heel and bounding up the stairs. Seconds later they heard her bedroom door slam.

"Oh, Cal, that poor kid. Was it bad for her?"

She finally got herself under control. "Yeah, Bobbi. It was hell for her all day. I've gotta go talk to her."

She nodded. "If anyone can cheer her up, it's you."

"By the way, I'm spending the night, Bobbi," Callie called as she climbed the stairs.

She knocked on Katie's door, and when she didn't respond, Callie walked in, seeing her sprawled across her bed. She sat next to her and ran her fingertips over her back. "Katie, I'm sorry for the rotten day you had. I know you suffered because of me. No one would ever do the things for me that you do."

Katie ignored her.

"I'm sorry I laughed. In the bathroom this morning you don't know how much I wanted to just grab you and take you outta there. I know you must have been thinking I didn't care, but that's not true. I wanted to hold you and protect you from everyone. Please talk to me."

Katie rolled over on her side and faced her. The humiliation in her eyes ripped Callie's heart wide open. "I'll never ask you to do anything like that again." She kissed her cheek. "I should have never asked you to do this in the first place."

Katie put her arms around Callie's neck, drawing her close. "You owe me big time for this one. Now I'll really be the laughing stock of school."

Callie looked into her eyes. "I owe you for so much already. I guess you'll have to keep me around for the rest of your life so I can make it up to you."

"That was decided the minute we met."

Chapter 17

Katie never adjusted to Callie's dating guys, no matter how many times Callie insisted it was necessary to throw people off the track of their relationship. They'd been together for almost two years now, and for the past six months they'd been almost inseparable as their love deepened and grew, taking them through the awkward stage of adolescence. She was glad that they went through their clumsy stages together. They both knew that they were fortunate and destined to spend their mortal and hopefully their eternal lives together, but just the same, Katie seemed leery of Randy North.

Callie loved Randy, but not in the way she loved Katie. Randy was easy to talk to, with a witty sense of humor, and he made her laugh. He was her best guy pal. She always enjoyed the time she spent with him, and since he lived in Carlton, she only saw him a couple of times a month, enabling her to spend the rest of the time with Katie. It was a perfect setup for them.

She'd been dating Randy for eight months, and their friendship was deepening. It was refreshing to date a boy who didn't have his clumsy hands all over her, trying to convince her to have sex with him. Randy never expected more than a few kisses, and even though she didn't want to, Callie obliged so he wouldn't suspect anything. They'd spend their time together laughing and joking, watching TV and sometimes going to the drive-in when the weather permitted. One night Randy became a little amorous, which was out of character for him, and before realizing what he'd done planted a large purple hickey on her neck. Neither of them knew about it until they stopped in the diner.

The whole crowd was there, but Callie knew they'd be leaving shortly since most of them had curfews. Stopping in after a date was a good way for her to be seen with Randy and not Katie eternally planted by her side, even though deep down she wished Katie had been the one with her at the drive-in.

Michelle, Debbie, Terry, Grace, and Dana were sitting together in a large booth. Debbie's sister Betty was at the counter with her boyfriend George. Michelle and Debbie rushed up to her.

"Where'd you guys go tonight?" Debbie asked.

"The drive-in. Randy wanted to see Clint Eastwood."

"I'll bet that's not all he saw," she smirked, pointing to Callie's neck.

Callie raised her eyes. "What are you talking about?"

Randy looked to where Debbie was pointing, then sheepishly met her gaze. "I'm sorry."

"You've got a hickey," Debbie squealed, loud enough for everyone to hear.

Callie ran to the restroom and over to the mirror with her friends at her heels. Her reflection showed a big purple splotch on her neck. "Shit," she mumbled. "How the hell can I get rid of it?"

"Your Mom's going to kill you," Dana said matter-of-factly.

Callie kept silent. She needed to think. She wasn't worried about her mother's reaction, but Katie's. What Katie would think disturbed her. How would she ever be able to explain this to her?

"I heard that a hairbrush helps," Debbie suggested. "You just keep brushing it."

Michelle handed her a brush. Even though it seemed silly, she had nothing to lose and hopefully everything to gain. She stroked it gently at first, then harder, but all it appeared to do was make her neck burn and throb. She grabbed her bottle of liquid make up from her purse and dabbed some on as the others looked on, offering useless tidbits of advice. Her tension mounted. The blotch was still visible through the makeup.

"It's too bad it's not winter. You could wear a turtleneck sweater," Michelle reasoned.

Callie groaned. "I'll think of something." Right now she just wanted to be left alone. As soon as the gang went home, she'd cut the date with Randy short. She had plans with Katie tomorrow, so she'd have to either receive a miracle overnight or devise a way to hide her neck from Katie, and that wouldn't be an easy feat.

All night she periodically brushed her neck, then about four o'clock in the morning fell into a fitful sleep. In the morning she bounded out of bed and rushed to the mirror. The hickey was still there in all its ugly glory. She would never understand how some girls strutted around with them all over their necks, acting like it was a cherished medal.

She rummaged through her dresser drawers and pulled out a turtleneck sweater. Today was supposed to be in the high sixties. How could she pull this off? How could she prevent Katie from seeing it? She knew she had to tell her. Even if she did manage to hide it from her for a few days, her friends would certainly rib her about it in school on Monday. Then Katie might think Callie was doing more than making out with Randy and would be convinced that she was hiding things from her. She needed to stall for a little time until she could explain it to her. She'd make sure that they avoided the usual hangouts today in case they ran into someone they knew or who knew about the hickey.

***

Katie's eyes grew wide when she saw the turtleneck. "Kinda warm for that, Cal."

Callie started to put her love beads around her neck. Katie had given them to her last Christmas. Katie was wearing the beads she'd given her, too.

Katie came up behind her, gently lifting her hair. "Let me help."

"I've got it," Callie quickly said, throwing the beads over her head.

"I can't believe you did that. Aren't you afraid of messing up your hair?" she teased.

She'd been with Callie long enough to know how picky she was about her makeup and hair. Callie made up a fast excuse. "I don't feel well."

Her eyes clouded as she softly touched Callie's cheek. Callie felt like shit for lying to her.

"Why don't we just hang around here today, then?" Katie suggested.

She carefully and strategically held a strand of her hair to obscure Katie's view of her neck. "Want to see a movie, or better yet, hang out at your house? We'd have more privacy," she said with a sly grin.

She frowned. "Do you feel well enough to walk?"

She nodded.

They walked slowly, Callie's only consolation being that since Katie always insisted on walking on the outside, she was now to the left of her and the hickey was on her right. Callie was safe for a while, at least.

Later they lay on pillows on the floor, watching westerns on TV. Callie tried to find a way to tell Katie, but nothing she came up with sounded right, and because Katie believed Callie was sick, she walked over to the Tastee Delight, returning thirty minutes later with burgers and fries. Callie was ashamed of her deception as she watched Katie set their dinner out on the coffee table. They ate while watching another old western movie.

Every so often Katie reached over and touched her cheek. "Sure you're really okay?"

Callie saw the worry in her eyes, and she felt queasy with guilt as she nodded. Making up being sick was only compounding the situation, and she had to tell her the truth right now. "Katie, I have to tell you something."

"What?" She laid her hand on Callie's arm.

Before Callie could say another word, Bobbi burst through the door, loaded down with shopping bags. Katie ran to her, pulling the grocery bags from her arms. Callie knew the chance was gone. She'd have to tell her later.

When they were finally in Katie's bedroom Katie reached for her, and Callie was careful not to let her push her hair back. "Let's turn out the light and climb into bed," she suggested. Once they were snuggled together, she'd tell her.

"I thought maybe you'd want to read or write for awhile."

She shook her head and watched as Katie turned the light switch off. Feeling her warm soft body next to her own quickly aroused her. She touched Katie's cheek.

Katie held her hand. "Are you feeling better?"

"When I'm here alone with you," she whispered. Her honest intention to tell her disappeared as they shared gentle kisses that soon ignited their passion.

Afterward Callie laid her head on Katie's shoulder as Katie held her in her arms. They were content and at peace in the afterglow of their lovemaking, and she couldn't shatter their golden moment. Minutes later they drifted into a restful slumber.

***

Callie awoke to find Katie staring down at her. She raised herself up on her elbows and softly brushed her lips against Katie's. Katie didn't respond, but her eyes revealed unmistakable pain. "Katie, what's wrong?"

She swallowed hard. "Why didn't you tell me...your neck?"

Callie sat up and enclosed her in her arms. "I was going to tell you. Honest I was."

She lowered her eyes. "What about being sick yesterday?"

She let her breath out slowly, her heart pounding wildly. "I'm so sorry, Katie. I didn't know how to tell you so I was stalling for time. I know I should have told you right away. " She wished the proper words would come to mind, but they seemed to elude her, and her reasoning sounded feeble and phony even to her own ears. She couldn't stand the pain Katie was in, and what made it worse was that Callie knew she was to blame for inflicting it on her.

Katie took a ragged breath. "I don't understand. Was it Randy, or were you with some other girl the other night?"

Callie shook her head. "No, it was Randy. He was horsing around. It didn't mean anything. Honest!"

She took another breath. "Did you fuck him?" she asked in a cracked voice.

"No! Of course not. How could you even ask me that?" she asked disgustedly.

She bit her bottom lip as her tears began to fall.

Callie put her arms around her, rubbing her back and planting affectionate kisses on her cheeks, tasting her salty tears. She swallowed the lump in her throat. "You're the only one, Katie. You know that."

"I can't stand the thought of you and Randy making out. I don't like knowing that he touches you and kisses you."

"You know why I date him, Katie. But I swear to you that nothing has or will ever happen between Randy and me. I only want to be with you. God, I love you so much! I can't wait till we can get the hell out of here so we can be together all the time. I hate being away from you. I only want to be with you always."

"Forever," she whispered.

"You know it's forever."

Chapter 18

Callie's mother confronted her when she got home from work one day, taking her by complete surprise. She wondered what she'd done now. Or maybe her mother just needed to take her frustrations out on her again. As long as she knew she was going to be with Katie all night, she could handle whatever ridiculous accusations her mother had against her now.

"I won't tolerate your rudeness to anyone in this house," she ranted. "You have no right to say anything about who comes in or out of this house!"

Callie shrugged. "I don't know what you're talking about."

"You know perfectly well who I'm talking about. Uncle Ned has been good to you kids. He's upset that you barely give him the time of day anymore."

"He's not my uncle." She wished she could tell her what her precious friend had done to her. Sometimes she believed her mother already knew and kept a blind eye to it.

"Ever since 'that girl' moved here, you've been nothing but a smart aleck. She's a bad influence on you."

"You know for two years you've been calling her 'that girl'. She has a name. It's Katie. Remember? I introduced you to her two years ago."

"Don't get smart with me!"

Callie scowled. "I should just move in with her. It's not like anyone cares about me here! At least Katie and Bobbi care about me."

She swiftly brought the back of her hand across Callie's cheek. "Keep it up and you'll be forbidden to go near her. I knew she was trouble the first time I laid eyes on her."

"Think whatever you want to," Callie snapped as she stomped up the stairs, her hand rubbing her sore cheek.

***

Bobbi laughed at Callie's dance. When she pulled Katie to her feet, Bobbi clapped her hands in time to the music blaring from the radio. "Come on, Katie, get the beat," she shouted.

Katie grinned. "I would, but every time I get one move down, Cal moves too fast and throws in a new one."

Callie grabbed Katie's hands. "Whew! I'm beat. I need to rest a minute." She pulled Katie to the couch and plopped down next to her.

"It's nice to have you here tonight, Callie. I'm surprised you're not at the dance club."

She smiled sheepishly. "Not tonight. Katie doesn't like going, and I promised her I'd quit going so much." She winked at Bobbi, then said in a whisper she knew was loud enough for Katie to hear, "She's jealous."

Katie's mouth dropped open. "No I'm not…Well, not all the time. Only when you dress in mini skirts. Okay, so I don't like the way everybody looks at you."

Callie chuckled. "I'd still rather be here." She wiped the perspiration from her brow. "Wow, it's hot in here."

Bobbi laughed. "That's because of all the dancing you've been doing." She leaned closer. "Callie, what's that on your cheek?"

She put her hand to her face. "Oh that's nothing. I bumped into something tonight when I was getting ready to come over."

"You'd better be careful, honey. It looks like someone punched you."

Katie looked closely at her cheek. "Let me see." She took a tissue and gently wiped the perspiration from Callie's face, along with her makeup.

Callie saw the pained look that instantly came into Katie's eyes as Katie softly ran her fingertips over the purplish bruise. "I'm so clumsy some times," Callie said feebly.

"What happened?" Katie asked. "You couldn't have done this by running into something."

Her eyes narrowed. "It's no big deal."

Bobbi walked over to her. "Honey, you're not being..."

She shook her head. "No, he hasn't come near me since Katie warned him."

"Then what?"

She gave a weak laugh. "I told you it's nothing...really."

"Who did this to you, Callie? Don't lie to me, please. It was no accident," Bobbi said firmly.

She looked down at her hands, then back up into Bobbi's warm, sympathetic eyes. "My mother," she said in a barely audible voice.

Katie was instantly on her feet. "Dammit."

Callie looked at Katie's red face. "It's okay."

Katie grabbed Bobbi's arm. "Mom, can't Callie move in here with us?" she implored.

Bobbi patted her shoulder. "Honey, I'd love nothing better than for Callie to live with us, but do you seriously think your mother would go for it, Callie?"

"Probably not." She sighed heavily without telling them the run-in she'd had earlier with her mother. "I could just leave." Her eyes searched Bobbi's. "She couldn't do anything about it if I just left."

Bobbi chewed her bottom lip. "Callie, your mother could do a lot." She was thoughtful for a minute. "Honey, I could get into trouble. You're still considered a minor. If anyone found out about you and Katie, I could be charged for allowing you two to be together in my home in a sexual relationship."

"But no one knows what Cal and I are doing, and besides, what's the big deal? We love each other."

"Honey, whether anyone knows what goes on under this roof or not, it'll still give them something to gossip about."

Callie's eyes brimmed with tears. "I thought you understood and supported us, Bobbi," she said in a broken voice. "I want to stay here with you and Katie."

"Oh, honey, I do!" she exclaimed scooping both girls into her arms. "I'll do anything in my power to keep you two together, but moving in here against your mother's wishes is not the answer."

"If you let me stay here, I promise I won't cause you any trouble. I'm sixteen now. I'll cook and clean and I'll get another job besides my school job to help out," Callie pleaded. "I just want to get away from my family. I only feel alive when I'm with Katie."

Bobbi blinked hard. "Callie, I'd take you in with us in a heartbeat, sweetie, but you know what would happen."

She lowered her eyes. "I know. But my mother doesn't care about me. You'd think she'd be glad to get rid of me."

Katie's jaw twitched. "Well, then, you'll just stay here more often until we're of age and can be together."

Bobbi watched Katie protectively move closer to Callie. "You two have been through so much these past two years, and I know it hasn't been easy."

Katie smiled. "Yeah, but every day it's getting closer to us being together forever."

"I know how you two feel about each other, but you have to remember there are some people who are never going to understand or accept your love no matter how much you try to convince them. I hate to keep reminding you of that, but it's unfortunately just the way it is."

Callie nodded. "We know, and it's hard sometimes. Especially when Katie was sick and I was so scared, but couldn't lean on my friends."

Bobbi patted her hand. "Yes, but if it hadn't been for your

love and devotion I don't know how Katie or I would have gotten through it. And I certainly don't know where you got the stamina."

Callie grew serious. "I didn't think of anything but how I would feel if anything happened to her. I was so scared."

Katie smiled at her.

"I know you were, sweetie. I could see it in your eyes and when you'd refuse to leave Katie's bedside."

"I love her, and I'd do it again if I had to." She grabbed Katie's hand.

Chapter 19

Callie lay on her bed, staring up at the ceiling. "School's in two weeks."

"Yeah," Katie answered with a grin. "It's been a great summer."

Callie grabbed her hand. "Yeah, even if I did miss Woodstock."

Her eyes clouded. "I'm sorry. It's just that I would've worried so much if you went."

"I told you that you could have come with me. We could've had a blast."

"Well, number one, I didn't know the people you were riding with, not that you knew them well either. And number two, you know I'm not into that kind of thing."

"I know, but I love you anyway."

"Are you still upset that you missed it?"

She tossed her head. "Sort of. It's probably gonna go down in musical history." She saw the guilt come into Katie's eyes. "But if I had to choose between you and Woodstock, you know there's no contest. You're more important."

She smiled. "Thanks." She brushed her lips against Callie's. "I've got to go."

Callie abruptly sat up. "Go where? Why? I thought you were spending the night."

"I can't. My Mom wants me home by ten."

"You didn't say anything earlier. Call her and tell her that you're spending the night. She won't care if you stay over; she never cares when we're together."

She shook her head. "No, it's important, Cal. Something's wrong. I've never seen my Mom so upset. I know I should've told you earlier, but we were having such a good time I didn't want to ruin it."

Callie frowned. "Then I'll go with you and spend the night there. I'll hang out in your room so you and Bobbi can talk privately. She won't mind."

"She said I needed to be alone tonight. There's something major going on. She's been acting funny for a couple of days."

"Is she mad at me for something?"

"Oh no! She loves you, Cal. You know that. She just needs to talk to me about something. I'm sure it'll end up being no big deal. You know how she can be sometimes." She made a face. "I'll call you. Be by the phone about midnight...no, why don't you call me instead? Then your Mom won't be bitching about the phone ringing so late."

"Well, okay, but I wish I could go with you. I hope everything's okay with your Mom. Tell her I'll see her tomorrow and I'll show her my latest dance moves." She saw the worried look in Katie's eyes. "I love you, Katie. Everything will be okay." She kissed her goodbye.

"I love you, Cal." She squeezed her hand. "You know I always will."

$$***$$

Bobbi paced back and forth, wringing her hands. "We have no choice, Katie."

Tears streamed from Katie's eyes. "Why, Mom? At least let me call Callie. What will she think? I don't understand any of this."

Bobbi swallowed the lump in her throat. "No, honey. You can't write or call Callie ever. It's better this way. I'm sorry, baby."

"Why? Better for who? She's not going to know what happened! I can't leave her," she cried. "I'm going back to Callie's right now. I'm not going to leave her."

"Katie, please listen to me for a minute." She wiped the tears from her own eyes. "If we don't go, you'll never be able to see Callie again anyway. Callie will be sent away."

"But Mom, Callie's not going to know what happened. How's she going to feel? How would you feel if it happened to you, and the person you were in love with and who was in love with you just disappeared one day without a word?"

"Honey, someday you can tell her."

"How can I tell her when I don't even know myself? I don't see why I can't tell her we're moving so she can come and visit."

"Honey, I told you some people would never understand the relationship between you and Callie."

"Just because Callie and I love each other we have to be ripped apart? It's not fair!"

"A lot of things in life aren't fair, Katie. But I'll help you get through this. I love you, and I'll always love Callie as my own, too."

Katie threw her arms around her mother's neck. "It hurts so bad, Mom," she cried. "Why does this have to happen? We didn't hurt anybody."

"I know, honey," Bobbi soothed as the anger against intolerant bigots boiled inside of her.

***

At midnight Callie picked up the phone and dialed Katie's number. She waited patiently, but after several rings figured that she and Bobbi must have gone out to do something. She sat by the phone and for the next two hours periodically dialed the number, becoming concerned but knowing Katie would have a logical explanation. She reluctantly went to bed, but tossed and turned most of the night, awakening a little after eight in the morning.

She jumped out of bed and hurriedly dressed, then raced to the phone and dialed Katie's number, waiting for either her or Bobbi's bubbly voice to come over the line. When she still received no answer, a fear in the pit of her stomach began to gnaw at her.

She had to go to Katie's and make sure everything was all right. She couldn't stay home waiting for a call that might not come. All sorts of macabre images flooded her mind. She pictured Katie and Bobbi lying bleeding on the road somewhere, or murdered in their beds by some escaped psycho. She half-ran and half-walked to Katie's, gulping for air when she reached the apartment. She knocked on the door, then put her ear close to it, but heard nothing from the other side. She knocked again, only much harder this time. She impatiently looked around the courtyard for any sign of either of them.

A neighbor from next door peeked her head out of her screen door. "They're not home," she called to Callie.

Callie nodded. "Thanks. I'll just wait here for a little while till they get back."

The woman shook her head. "I'm afraid you're going to have a pretty long wait then. They aren't coming back."

Callie's heart froze. She looked at the woman, unable to speak.

"They moved out last night. In the middle of the night truck came right up to the door, and in about an hour they were all packed up and gone."

"Where to?" Callie hoarsely asked.

She shrugged. "Who knows? They mostly kept to themselves. Nobody knows where they went. That's the way it is around here with some of them…just a stopping off place till something better comes along. They were nice quiet people, though. Hope the next bunch is as quiet as they were."

Callie stood on her tiptoes, peering into the kitchen window. The room was barren. Her lips trembled as she backed away from the apartment. Her mind refused to believe that Katie was gone. No, they'd just moved somewhere else, she tried in vain to convince herself as she slowly walked in a daze back to her own house. Katie would call with the exciting news. She knew she would. It was a surprise Bobbi had planned for her, and later they'd invite Callie over to see their wonderful new home.

Callie stood in the kitchen doorway. "Any messages for me?" she asked, her own voice sounding far away.

Her mother looked at her strangely but said nothing, only shook her head and went back to her chores.

Callie slowly walked up the stairs to her bedroom, then silently closed the door. She sat on the edge of her bed as a crushing pain tore through her chest, leaving her deadened and so vastly empty. "Katie!" she sobbed. "No, you wouldn't desert me." She climbed into her bed and curled up into a fetal position, closed her eyes and stretched her hand to the space next to her. The space that Katie always occupied. When she opened her eyes, she'd find out that it was all just a horrible nightmare, and Katie would be there where she belonged. She took a shuddering breath and forced herself to open her eyes. She was alone. She stared at the empty space as memories of the love she and Katie shared came flooding back to haunt her. Katie's essence permeated the room. She buried her face in the sheets, smelling Katie there. She squeezed her eyes shut, and Katie's image grinned at her with that half-crooked smile that had so endeared Katie to her heart.

She cried out with the intense suffocating pain. Nothing would ever be the same again. She willed herself to die; death would be easier than this slow, painful lesion eating away at her. *No*, she thought, *death wasn't an option. What if Katie came back?* She knew that Katie would find a way; she had to. Callie let the tears pour from her eyes, washing down her cheeks and silently falling on the pillow. Katie was her best friend, lover and soul mate. How would she find the strength to face each day once again alone?

Callie spent the following weeks in a mental fog as she waited for a letter or phone call. As each day turned into the next, her hope slowly faded along with all of her dreams. Nothing would ever be the same again. How could destiny be so cruel as to bring Katie and her together if only to separate them? She looked at her finger, the one Katie had pricked so long ago, and remembered their pledge, "Always together, now and through eternity." *Someday*, she thought, *I'll see you again someday.*

Chapter 20

PRESENT

Callie never did find out what happened to Katie, and as the weeks turned into years, still not one day went by that she didn't think about her, and often wondered if Katie ever thought about her.

Callie denied her true sexual identity for years and succumbed to living her lifestyle the way everyone said she should, but deep down inside knew that she was only lying to herself; consequently she had two failed marriages, several loveless relationships, but her two beautiful children gave her the hope and renewal she needed. She wished she could have shared their births with Katie and they could have celebrated together this wonderful miracle of new life.

As the years wore on her true nature battled to be set free. The time had come, and if she were ever to find any happiness again in her life she had to surrender herself. Her memories of Katie and all they had shared couldn't be denied. She needed to remember how sweet, innocent and natural their love had been. It was time to close this chapter in her life and forge ahead in her pursuit of happiness, but no matter how long she lived, she'd never get over her loss of Katie. Katie'd always remain a part of her, and in her heart she'd always dwell, her soul mate, her best friend and her lover.

THE END